All rights reserved

The characters and events portray(
similarity to real persons, living or
intended by the author.

No part of this book may be reproc
system, or transmitted in any form or by any means, electronic,
mechanical, photocopying, recording, or otherwise, without express
written permission of the publisher.

Lesley Bown has asserted her right under the Copyright, design and
Patents Act, 1988 to be identified as the author of this work.

© 2024 Lesley Bown.

Angela, This is my friend's latest book set in Weston — do you see me in one of the characters maybe 😊 xx.

Thanks to Ann, Jane, Jean and Mike

WHATEVER YOU WANT

by

Lesley Bown

PROLOGUE

It is 1996.

Charles and Diana are finally heading for divorce.

John Major is Prime Minister.

Mobile phones cost an arm and a leg.

The internet is a clunky and rarely used dial-up system.

And two middle aged couples are coming to the end of the road.

SATURDAY APRIL 13th 1996

Raymond Boyles settled himself in front of the TV with a contented sigh. Aston Villa were on *Match of the Day*, he had a can of beer and a packet of pork scratchings and his wife was away. It didn't get more perfect than that. Football was his passion, and although it had been many years since he'd made the trek back to the Midlands to watch his favourite team in person, he still considered himself to be the Villans' number one fan.

It was nearly half time and, so far, a nil-nil draw. That didn't bother Ray, goals were exciting but he was a true aficionado, a man who appreciated the finer points of play, the subtle strategies and tactics.

'Go on, my son,' he screamed, as a forward broke free and sprinted for the goal, but he was toppled by a sliding tackle and ended in an inglorious heap. Ray grinned happily. Not at the poor player, who was now being attended by the man with the wet sponge, but because he could scream freely at the TV without fear of his wife's disapproval.

Margaret was away, enjoying a spa weekend of pampering that Ray had given her as a birthday gift. An inspired choice, since it achieved the rare double feat of making both of them happy.

The player was now hobbling pitifully, shaking his head and indicating that he would heroically continue to play (just as well thought Ray, the substitute's bench was full of rubbish). He allowed himself a contented belch (bliss to be able to belch as much as he wanted, not to mention farting whenever it took his fancy) and popped open the can.

Somewhere in the far distance a bell rang. It was the doorbell and Raymond ignored it. The shop was closed so it was probably kids messing around. It was unlikely to be someone in urgent need of a face pack or a leg wax.

The shop was a beauty parlour and hairdresser, the only shop at the end of a row of Victorian terraced houses. It had originally been a corner shop but when the supermarkets took over there was no longer any need for it. Ray and Margaret lived in the rooms above and behind the shop, which were not designed as accommodation but rather as storerooms or, if really pressed, offices. However the kitchen installed by previous owners when staff coffee breaks became mandatory made living there possible, and saved them a lot of money. As soon as they moved in they hived off a space to create a downstairs shower room which doubled up as a tax deductible 'unique extra for the benefit of our clients' and which the clients never used, possibly because they didn't know it was there, hidden as it was behind the curtain that separated the shop from the living quarters. The small sitting room and two bedrooms were above the shop, up a narrow flight of stairs. There was no garden, but a yard at the back had access for parking a car.

The whistle blew for half time, and Ray cleared the coffee table of the remains of his supper (takeaway curry, another rare treat) and padded down to the kitchen to tidy up. Even though his wife was a hundred miles away he could still feel her looking over his shoulder. She rarely cooked but she did like a clean and tidy kitchen. He was bending to retrieve a chocolate eclair from the freezer when he heard the doorbell again, this time with the added sounds of someone banging on the door.

With a sigh he pushed aside the curtain and went through to the darkened shop, wondering what would be the quickest way to get those kids to sling their hooks so he could get back to the football. But there was only one small hooded figure silhouetted against the streetlight. He unfastened the security locks and opened the door the merest crack, but before he could say 'time you were tucked up in bed, sunbeam' the figure burst past him, into the shop, somehow managing to drop a suitcase and seize the chocolate eclair.

'Oh Ray, Ray,' it said through mouthfuls of frozen cream, 'I's come to you in my hour of darkest need. Has you got any more of these choc ices?'

'No,' Ray said crossly, 'that was the last one and I… hang on just one little minute, what are you doing here and now I come to think of it, who are you?'

'It's me,' said the woman, because now she had thrown back the hood, Ray could see a mass of unkempt curls and a plump little face. 'I'm in direst need of a place of refuge, ooh maybe Margie could make us some toast?'

'Margaret's not here,' said Ray, running his mind over all the short curly badly groomed women amongst Margaret's friends and coming up empty. There wasn't one who would wear an oversized red hoodie with a pair of baggy bright pink joggers and orange slippers with woolly bobbles on the front. He opened the shop door wide 'so I'll say goodnight and…'

But the woman had walked past him into the back of the shop.

'I know, let's phone for a pizza. I hasn't had pizza for years, you know how Steve don't like it so we never has it. Oh Ray, when I think what I's sacrificed to make that man happy, and how he's repaid me, he always was ungrateful but I loves him Ray, he's my soulmate, leastways he was my soulmate…'

'Dilys!' Ray gasped, as the penny dropped, 'is it really you?'

'Of course it's me innit,' said Dilys, who had found the phone and was busily dialling a number she clearly knew by heart, 'let's get a Beef Feast with extra cheese.'

******

About fifty miles away (geography had never been Ray's strong point) Margaret was getting ready for bed. It was a slow process, a ritual that involved much folding of clothes, laying out of jewellery, cosseting of contact lenses, multiple creams for multiple purposes and of course the settling of her wig on its folding travel wig stand. She was taking it step by step, on autopilot because she had much to think about. It had been a very strange day.

It had started well enough, with a peaceful drive across the Somerset levels to the remote country house hotel, which looked imposing enough in the early spring sunshine. Reluctantly she had to admit she was impressed. It was rare for Raymond to go to any trouble over her birthday. Usually it was garage flowers or some perfume he'd picked up at the market.

Normally of course she worked on a Saturday but things weren't normal at the moment. The salon had been sold, Ray and Margaret were taking early retirement and he had convinced her to seize the opportunity to have a weekend to herself. He had contrived to suggest that these events didn't come up very often without actually mentioning that he'd seen it in the local paper as a half price special offer.

'This is it, Margaret,' he had said to her, 'this is the future we've worked for. Instead of you running round after the clients, let someone else do the work while you lie back and enjoy being pampered. It's our turn. We've earned it.'

Check-in went smoothly, and she found herself in a large comfortable room, with a view across the lawns, and a most satisfactory en-suite bathroom. An en-suite was on Margaret's lengthy wish list and she took mental notes of this one, enjoying the grandeur of the space but thinking, as usual, that minimalist white decor reminded her too much of a public swimming pool. She would at the very least have chosen colour for the bathmat and towels, matching it of course to the lavatory paper. Green she thought, less common than blue and more tasteful than pink. She discounted apricot, which was the dominant colour in the shop decor and as a result she'd pretty much had enough of it.

It was only when she had unpacked and settled into the armchair by the window to read the programme that puzzlement set in. Clearly the staff, always the weak spot in any organisation, had left her the wrong paperwork. She phoned down to Reception and asked to be sent the correct literature, pertaining to the spa weekend. She was told there was no spa weekend. She insisted that there was, and she, Margaret Boyles, was booked onto it. She was told that no, she Margaret Boyles, was booked onto the Women's Empowerment weekend and that the introductory session would start in ten minutes. Would she please bring with her the timetable and checklist of sessions and workshops with her preferences ticked.

Just how Raymond had been able to see an advert headed 'Women's Empowerment' and read that as 'Spa' was unfathomable, but typical of the man. However, since she had been persuaded to close the salon for the day against her better judgement she was determined to have his money's worth. She hastily threw on her jacket, ticked a few random boxes and ran down to the Conference Suite.

And how glad she was that she'd ignored best friend Barbara's advice to 'wear something comfortable, no one dresses up for a spa.' Margaret always preferred to dress up, and so was wearing her scarlet jacket over a navy dress, and vertiginous heels. She found herself in a room full of woman of all shapes, sizes and dress codes.

The day was a dizzying succession of talks, workshops and 1-2-1 sessions with Empowerment Coaches, finished off with a grand five course dinner. Food hadn't interested Margaret for many years but she deeply regretted not packing her little black dress and diamanté studs. Luckily she did have a large silk embroidered pashmina in her case so she draped that over the navy dress, and she put on some false eyelashes.

She peeled them off now and put them carefully in their box. Somehow it looked like they were winking at her. Chin up Margaret they were saying, you're as good as that lot any day, better actually, you need to release your inner demon like that hypnotist was saying (she had hypnotised everyone in the room and told them all they could be winners).

Still, Margaret couldn't understand why she felt so outclassed. They all seemed to be doing better than her. They didn't need Empowering! And yet at the same time they were all so ordinary. There was that overweight woman with the frizzy hair and the high complexion. How much better she'd look with a de-frizz and the right makeup to tone down her high colour. And who'd have thought she was the owner of a successful builders' merchants, providing employment, apparently, for her entire family, a husband and four sons who all danced meekly to her tune. And those two hippie types in handmade natural-dyed jumpers and waist length matted hair, running a gift shop in Glastonbury with a massive turnover. They shut the shop for a month every winter and went travelling in Nepal or Indonesia, holidaying and buying new stock. How did they get all that money just from selling trinkets!

And yet I, Margaret thought, as she fastened her sleeping turban over her head, the only fully groomed woman in the room, have been struggling with a back street beauty parlour that barely pays its way. She attached the chin strap, adjusted it so that it would hold back her possible double chin without choking her, and climbed into bed, determined that tomorrow she would show those women that she too was a person of substance.

******

Dilys had finished the pizza, she ate most of it since Ray could only manage a small slice on top of his earlier meal. They'd eaten in front of the second half of the football although Ray couldn't really follow the match due to Dilys's incessant chatter. He'd had plenty of practice at zoning out Margaret's nagging but Dilys's voice was quite different and somehow inserted itself into his ear and distracted him, even though he was trying not to pay any attention to the content of her monologue. It wasn't that she was shrill, far from it. Margaret was shrill, but Dilys had a voice that was low and sweet and somehow compelled you to listen. He really, really needed to enjoy the rest of his blissfully solitary weekend. She had to go.

'Right then,' he said as she scraped the last few crumbs out of the box with her finger, 'how about we call you a cab. Or do you want to phone Steve to come and fetch you home?' She stared at him, aghast.

'I in't going home,' she said, 'and I in't phoning Steve. I told you how he broke my heart, and he took that broken heart Ray, and he stamped all over it, and he took all them little pieces and…'

'Yes, yes,' Ray interrupted before she could properly get going again, 'but you can't stay here, not with Margaret being away.'

'Ray, don't be daft. We're old friends innum, known each other since forever. I'll curl up on the couch, I won't be no trouble. Please Ray, pleeeeze.' She was about to cry, he could tell. He gave in.

'Oh alright,' he said, 'you can have the spare room. I'll go and clear the bed off. We're getting ready to move you know, so I've been having a sort out.'

'Ooh ta Ray, lovely job. Where you going to then? 'Ere, good job you didn't move any sooner, else I'd never have found you, boy I bet Margie's excited, lot of work though, moving, all that packing and unpacking and suchlike, I remember when them next door moved in, two vans they had, packed to the gills, and it's only a little house, can't think where they put it all…'

Ray escaped to the spare room. He was beginning to have some sympathy for Steve.

******

And a couple of miles away on the other side of town Steve was working methodically through his own nightly routine. It did not involve wig stands and chin straps. First he went out of the back door and checked the padlock on his shed, counting 'one, two, three' under his breath as he tugged it. Back in the kitchen he locked and bolted the door ('one, two, three'), he checked all round the room, tightened the hot and cold taps and switched off the special gas isolator tap next to the cooker. In the lounge-diner he put his hand on the back of the TV to check it had cooled down. He checked the remote controls were safely on the coffee table, because he'd heard about the person whose sofa caught fire when the remote got jammed between the cushions and the battery overheated from the constant pressure on the On button. Then he locked the front door (a final 'one, two, three'). He didn't bolt it in case Dilys was ready to come home, although past experience told him she'd be at her sister's for at least one night. He turned off the hall light and went upstairs to the bathroom. Only five minutes later he was in bed, stretched out carefully on his side. He switched off the light and instantly fell asleep.

SUNDAY APRIL 14th

Margaret woke up nice and early and was first down to breakfast, fully made up and not a hair out of place. Her dreams had all been of the other clients on the course - or were they customers maybe? Or students? Whatever they were every one of them was a woman and every one of them needed a makeover. She could see the frizzy haired woman with gently relaxed waves and a flattering dye job. The two hippies needed proper haircuts and a deep facial cleanse to stop them looking so grubby. Even the course leader, who at least was smartly dressed in a black skirt suit with a crisp white shirt, would benefit from a having her eyebrows plucked and a more subtle shade of blusher. There was still time to sort these women out, before the business finally closed. It could be her swan song.

She placed a little pile of the business cards ('Aphrodite's Hair and Beauty' in the salon's tasteful shade of apricot) discreetly on the serving table, next to the cooked breakfast menu, and sat herself in the corner with a yoghurt and an apple, watching the others struggle in, some only half dressed and the two hippies of course with no proper makeup at all, just black stuff round their eyes. It wasn't a time problem because they must have spent ten minutes at least dealing with all their bangles and scarves. No, they must prefer to look as if they'd gone ten rounds with Muhammed Ali. Just before the breakfast service closed the overweight woman came running in, wrapped in a towelling dressing gown and with her hair standing out like a halo round her head, and ordered 'a full English and don't forget the fried bread'.

Not one of them though picked up a business card, so on her way out Margaret quietly scooped them up. Despondency settled on her like a cloud.

****

Ray was feeling something similar. Sunday had started OK, he slept well and woke up ready for a long quiet day of nothing very much but definitely including a pint and a pie at the pub down the road. He padded naked down the hallway, scratching various bits that seemed to need it and planning on a nice long shower, but at the top of the stairs he heard a noise and froze. Someone was in the kitchen! Margaret must have come home early!

But tuneless singing floated up the stairs
Tanya, Tanya, Tanya, Tanyaaaaaa

I'm beggin of ya please don't take my man.

In a rush it all came back to him. Dilys. Dilys and her broken heart and apparently a passion for Country and Western that hadn't faded over the years. There had definitely been something about a Tanya, in amongst all the stuff about broken hearts and forgotten anniversaries, plus something about chips, quite where the chips fitted in he wasn't sure, but he'd already learned that wherever Dilys was there was sure to be food somewhere in the vicinity.

Grabbing the fringed table cloth from Margaret's half round hall table he made himself more or less decent and headed downstairs.

And there was Dilys, in a long baggy t-shirt and, he fervently hoped, knickers, scoffing the last of Margaret's special no-cal breakfast cereal.

'Ere, Ray,' she said, 'ain't you got no proper breakfast? I can't get by on a bowl of crispy paper flakes.'

'Let me have my shower first,' he said, 'then we can scramble some eggs.'

And they did, they scrambled eggs, made toast, ate, cleared up, and all the while Dilys talked about a) broken hearts and b) what to have for lunch. Ray began to wonder if GBH of the earhole was actually a crime and not just a feeble joke because Dilys was apparently incapable of not talking. He was beginning to feel nostalgic for Margaret's frosty silences when the phone rang.

'If that's for I,' Dilys whispered, 'I ain't here, right?'

'Don't be daft, Dil, who even knows you're here?'

'It might be Steve, saying his heart is broken and begging me to come home'.

'But you said you didn't tell him where you were going.'

'Love finds a way Ray, love finds a way.'

Ray picked up the receiver.

'Aphrodite's Hair and Beauty... no I'm sorry, we're closed. No we don't have any late evenings. 'Bye.'

******

It had been an effort to sit through the first session of the morning, 'Can a business woman also be a feminist?' Margaret had never been interested in feminism so she pretended to listen while wallowing in gloom. Why haven't I done better in life she asked herself bitterly. I'm good at what I do, I've worked hard, what goes wrong? Why haven't I achieved more? Nothing goes wrong, said a little voice at the back of her head, nothing at all Margaret, but do you think perhaps Raymond has been holding you back all these years? Ah yes, Raymond, who couldn't even be bothered to read an advertisement properly. And now he thought they were ready for retirement. She shuddered, thinking of the empty years stretching ahead, with nothing to do but stare out of the window while Ray watched sport on TV or slipped out to the bookies.

'That was interesting, don't you think?' It was the fat woman, fully dressed now, sidling up to Margaret in the coffee break and interrupting her thoughts by shouting at her. Maybe she was deaf, deaf people did that, at least the old ladies who came for her OAPs Special did.

'Oh, yes, quite interesting, I suppose'

'I mean,' she continued, at full volume glancing quickly round her, 'on the one hand we are independent women demanding equality and on the other hand we can use our feminine wiles to help our businesses succeed.'

Margaret had heard something vaguely along those lines. She had no opinion, she'd never needed to be a feminist and she wasn't planning to start now. The woman glanced around again and dropped her voice.

'Er,' she said, 'I don't suppose you can help with, you know,' she dropped down to a whisper and Margaret had to lean forward 'you know, weight loss? Does that come under grooming? You said you did grooming.'

It did not come under grooming, which Margaret had mentioned when they were each called on to explain their role in life, but she was not about to lose a potential customer so she smiled sympathetically.

'I don't suppose you've ever had to worry about that,' the woman said sadly, 'but we're all big boned in my family. If only I could find the right diet.'

In truth weight loss did not come under the remit of a beauty parlour at all but Margaret was not going to admit to that. Nor would she admit to having had to worry about her weight having been a chubby child and a plump teenager. As far as she was concerned the answer was 'eat less and move more' but she quickly pressed a business card into the woman's hand and said 'call me, I'm sure we can help'. She already knew how she would shape the woman's hair to make her face look thinner, and maybe show her how to sculpt her cheeks with blusher.

******

Across town from Aphrodite's another phone was ringing. Steve carefully placed the hot iron on the heat proof mat at the end of the ironing board, picked up the receiver and said hello.

'Oh hi, dad, er, can you call us back? Just for a minute?'

'No, Cheyenne, I told you when you left, you has to pay your way.'

'I know you did but… oh never mind. Is mum there?'

'Er no, no, she's, er…' Steve found it difficult to lie, not for any moral reasons but because he had no imagination.

'Oh don't tell me she's done a bunk again. You had another spat didn't you?'

'Well, not as such…'

'You forgot your anniversary again didn't you?'

'Not exactly forgot…' To be honest, Steve wasn't entirely sure. It may have been one of their anniversaries (they had several, starting with the day they met, then their first date, then the day they got engaged, then their wedding day, and a raft of others that he could never remember) but it could have been something else, such as the business with Tanya that had somehow gotten out of hand.

'Sorry dad, this is costing me a fortune, I'll have to hang up and phone Aunty Phyllis, she always goes there when she's fed up doesn't she? Love you, byeeee.'

Steve put the phone carefully back in its cradle, picked up his steel ruler and went back to his ironing. He did like the folds in his handkerchiefs to be properly square.

******

Ray had begun to think that he'd slipped through a wrinkle in the space time continuum and was in some sort of time warp, a bit like *Back to the Future* or *Star Trek* maybe. He'd married Dilys and in this new world Margaret had presumably married her first boyfriend, Max Something, and Steve was probably a bachelor still living with his mum. The thought of Margaret stuck with boring old Max made him smile, and he could see Steve with a shopping trolley plodding behind his mum in the supermarket.

All this because Dilys had made herself so entirely at home. Ray had organised breakfast, but then she sort of took over. She had re-tuned the radio to something raucous, washed up, dried up and then scrubbed down the kitchen, all while shouting over the music so she could tell a long story that had something to do with metal detectorists finding a diamond ring in the Weston mud and how they returned it to the owner in Manchester and wasn't that a romantic thing to do since they coulda just sold it. Then she sat Ray at the table with a coffee and the paper and told him 'I'm gonna hoover upstairs, you stay there like a good boy and keep outta my way alright?'

Well, he thought, I'm not going to say no to someone else doing the cleaning for once, and he settled down with the Sports section. Eventually it went quiet upstairs and she reappeared with the laundry basket.

'Let me have my elevenses,' she said, 'then I'll give these sheets a seeing to. Where d'you keep the iron then? Is it a steam one? I got a lovely one, Steve bought it … oh!' And then she was weeping, and Ray fell out of the time warp back into the real world. But now he could see that maybe Steve had some compensation for the non-stop chatter.

******

This time Steve was in his shed when the cordless phone rang. It was a small shed and stuffed to the gills. Against the wall opposite the window was his workbench, and when the bench was clear he could lower a large hinged sheet of plywood down from the wall, so that it rested on the bench. It had all the track for his model railway permanently in place. Power for the railway and lights came from an extension cable trailing from the house and heat, when needed, from an ancient paraffin stove. He stored his tools under the bench in large plastic boxes and his locos and rolling stock, plus a selection of model buildings, on narrow shelves below the window. There was only just room for Steve himself to squeeze in. He longed for a permanent set-up without all the palaver of getting it out and putting it away, but the shed was the best he could do and he had grown to love it.

He carefully put down the tiny brush he was using to fill in the detail on his new station building and picked up the cordless phone, which was resting on its designated shelf to one side of the window. The signal barely reached this far into the garden so he could hardly hear the voice.

'Dil, is that you? You coming home?' he said.

'Dad, can you…'

'No.'

'Well she in't there, I couldn't get no answer from Aunty Phil so I phoned cousin Roger and he said his mum's in Torremolinos. Their house is all locked up, she ain't got a key has she?'

'I dunno,' Steve said, 'but I expect she's OK.'

'Dad! She could be sleeping on the streets!' Steve sighed.

'Alright, alright,' he said, 'I'll look into it.'

He'd spent twenty minutes carefully assembling everything he needed for his model making, and now he had to put it all away again and start looking for his runaway wife who was almost certainly perfectly fine. Really, he was not best pleased.

But once Steve committed to doing something, he did it properly. He began to pack a small rucksack with all the things one might need for finding a lost wife. Box of tissues because there would be tears when she was found. Flashlight, and spare batteries, for looking under hedges and down alleyways. Photo of Dilys for showing to people (he took the one from the sideboard, which was taken on her fifth birthday). Notebook and pen, for writing down their answers and any other clues. Local street map, so he could take the most efficient route without repeating himself (it didn't occur to him that she might be on the move). A note of the addresses of all their friends - the address book itself was too large for the rucksack, and also falling to bits.

Eventually he could postpone it no longer. He would need food and water. He would have to face the kitchen.

Steve had not always had a phobia of the kitchen. When he was first married he was determined to help Dilys. He didn't want her chained to the stove like his mother had been. But he soon learned they were completely unable to work together. He liked method, and a set of instructions that would work every time. Dilys found that boring.

He persisted, and bought a large and comprehensive recipe book, only to find that Dilys hated recipes. She rarely got to the end of the ingredients list before she had a better idea. In any case she preferred to throw things together and hope for the best. She was quite capable of saying to him 'I've made you a lovely omelette, 'course we ain't got no eggs but I think you'll like it.'

Sometimes he did like it, admittedly, but just as often he didn't. Her hit and miss cooking was always interesting and never predictable, which pretty much summed up their early years together. He stopped trying to help in the kitchen and settled for buying her every labour saving kitchen gadget known to man. Mostly they were never used, although the thermostatically controlled deep fat fryer did mean they could have chips without burning the house down. The electric bread slicer was still in pieces in his shed, because Dilys had somehow managed to jam it trying to slice a cabbage, which turned out to be too much for it.

The first time she took her broken heart off to her sister's, leaving him alone for a couple of nights, he thought he might as well learn to cook. Armed with the recipe book he set about creating the perfect shepherd's pie. But somehow his engineering and model making experience was no use to him at all. Laying out all your tools neatly before you started, assembling the ingredients and tidying up properly afterwards were all well and good but in between, well, mashed potato turned out lumpy, or watery, or both. Mince was a grey sludge with blobs of tomato puree floating in it. Chopped up carrot was like little orange bullets. On the second night he made beans on toast. He was out of the kitchen in five minutes which suited him fine. It had been beans on toast ever since whenever Dilys did a runner. Otherwise the kitchen was the place he scurried through on his way to the shed.

******

By Sunday evening most of the women had left the hotel, ready to get back to their businesses on Monday morning, but Ray had paid for Margaret to have the optional extra dinner, bed and breakfast and she was still determined to get his money's worth. No doubt he was looking forward to a lazy Monday morning without her. It would, she resolved, be the last time he skived. She was the only diner and she sat in solitary splendour, chewing on her Chef's Salad and thinking through everything she'd learned. It was a lot, almost too much to take in. In the end the weekend had been an eye opener and she was fired with enthusiasm for change. Her mind was whirling and a plan was beginning to emerge. Some of the details were still a little hazy but one thing was sure. Things were going to be different.

MONDAY APRIL 15th

'Of course, things are going to be different,' Ray said to Dilys as he cleared up breakfast and she wiped down the oilskin tablecloth. He was in a very cheerful mood. Not only had he got an early start and prepped for the Pensioner's Special Discount Afternoon before Dilys woke up, but this was the last time he would do it. Tomorrow he would go to the solicitor's office and sign the final paperwork. And then - freedom!

'Freedom,' he carried on, 'no more being tied to shop hours. No more customer service. No more customers! I'll be able to do whatever I flaming well want.'

He was distracted by the green tinge round Dilys's lips. It couldn't be... surely not... yes it was, it was avocado. She'd only gone and eaten the five avocado face packs he'd prepared for the pensioners, presumably while he was in the shower. On top of the porridge followed by bacon and eggs he'd cooked earlier. Plus the remains of their Sunday night curry, that she'd hoicked out of the bin.

At least she was a bit more decently dressed this morning. The t-shirt (motto: Love Is All You Need) was more than he could bear, since it had a tendency to ride up while simultaneously slipping off her shoulder, so he'd given her one of Margaret's frilly nylon negligées. It barely met in the middle across her stomach, but the belt seemed to be holding and at least it was long enough. (In fact it was too long, the hem trailed across the kitchen floor, picking up dust, and the cuffs were grubby from where she'd rummaged in the bin, but Ray wasn't the sort to notice anything like that).

Dilys sighed contentedly.

'Mmm,' she said, 'I does like a nice bit of avocado mousse.'

'I hate to rain on your parade, Dil,' Ray said, 'but those weren't mousses, those were face packs, face packs that I got ready to slap on to old lady's chops. So now I'd better go and mix up some more. And do get dressed there's a good girl, I don't want Margaret coming home to find you in her negligée.'

'Are you sure it's even Margie's?' Dilys said, 'her used to be ever so much fatter than I.'

'Well it ain't mine that's for sure,' Ray said, 'and she lost all that puppy fat years ago. Go on, get showered and sorted.'

Dilys ambled off to the shower room while Ray went through to the salon. He'd only just started on the new face packs, after a brief detour with the horseracing pages of the paper, when the shop door handle was rattled. He opened the door and Margaret stormed in.

'Raymond! Why is the closed sign up? Why aren't we open?'

'Oh don't fuss pet, you know we never open on a Monday morning. It's not as if we get any passing trade. And anyway tomorrow…'

'Don't you 'pet' me Raymond Boyles, and never you mind about tomorrow, things are going to be very different round here from now on, and we will most certainly be open on a Monday morning. And a Friday evening, it's incredible how many business opportunities we waste…'

'But Margaret, pet, sweetheart…'

'Sweethearting me won't get you any further than petting me you sad excuse for a man. There are going to be some changes around here, let me tell you, thank goodness we haven't gone public about closing the salon… what? What's that funny look for?'

'I may have mentioned it to the lads at the pub,' Ray said sheepishly.

'I don't think we have to worry about losing the business of your cronies, who by the way haven't been lads for many many years. No, I'm thinking we could be a one-stop shop for the modern career girl. All their hair and beauty needs in one relaxing session with complementary coffee and a luxury shower included. We really haven't been maximising our potential Raymond.'

The drive home had given her ample time for thought. She wasn't ready to retire! She was still in her prime, and she could turn the business around, she knew she could. She could see it now, the salon, somehow grown magically bigger, with its rows of stations for the staff she would need to do the hairdressing, a full time beautician in the cubicle waxing, pedicuring and manicuring all day long, happy customers relaxing in the tastefully appointed rest area, a glamorous receptionist on the front desk and she, Margaret, overseeing it all, organising, supervising and raking in the cash.

'I suppose the spa weekend has given you ideas,' Ray said glumly.

'Spa? Pah!' Margaret spat, 'it wasn't a spa at all Raymond, it was Women's Empowerment!'

Neither of them noticed Dilys, standing in the doorway clutching a toothbrush and still wearing the negligée, until she spoke.

'Has you got any toothpaste, Ray, I's run out.'

Margaret stared, horror struck, at the apparition. Then she found her voice if not her coherence.

'Who is this floozie?' she screamed, 'what is she doing here, as soon as my back is turned, mother always told me you… and oh dear heavens, she is wearing my second best negligée, it matches my… and look at the state of it, give it back at once you.. you…'

'Alright, alright,' Dilys said, 'I only borrowed 'im, I never thought to bring any night things seeing as how I was grappling with me broken 'eart.' She started to undo the belt, but Ray, who was fairly sure she was naked underneath, leapt forwards and held the edges of the negligée together.

'Margaret, this is…'

'Never mind the formal introductions, I'll deal with you later, you.. you… second rate Casanova, packing me off to that… and it wasn't even… give me my negligée and get out of here, whoever you are.'

And she opened the door with a dramatic flourish.

'Blimey, Marge, keep yer hair on, don't throw a hissy fit, I only come round here for a place of refuge in my time of need, seeing as how me 'usband is carrying on with that Tanya up the chip shop and me sister's in Torremolinos but if you can't help your best friend when she's lost in despair, well, fine, I'll sleep on the streets if I has to.'

Ray, with his well-honed instinct for self-preservation, started to edge away, but Margaret was staging a rapid recovery.

'Stand still you,' she barked at him, 'don't move a muscle.' She turned to Dilys. 'Now then, are you trying to tell me that you are Dilys, the same Dilys who never sends so much as a Christmas card? Best friend indeed!'

'I were busy weren't I, busy being pregnant, I must've been carrying on that last holiday we had, all that lovely sun and sea set me up a treat and I finally got a baby after all them years of trying. 'Course our mum put it down to her feeding me up like but…'

'And I suppose Steve was pregnant too was he? He could've made the effort surely.'

At the word 'Steve' Dilys launched herself at Margaret, wrapping her arms round her and burying her head in her bony chest.

'Oh, Marge, he's gone and broken me 'eart, again, I needs you in my hour of need, I needs your strength, your wisdom, your…'

'Yes,' said Margaret, disentangling herself, 'and you need my toothpaste too.'

She closed the shop door, took Dilys by the hand and headed for the shower room, mouthing at Ray 'I'll deal with you later.'

Squashed into the shower room with Dilys, Margaret quickly opened the cupboard and pulled out the tube of toothpaste, while simultaneously and surreptitiously checking her wig in the mirror. Yes it was still in place, so Dilys can't have meant anything by her remark about keeping your hair on. Or maybe she did. Was that innocent looking little face actually hiding a heart full of malice?

It was beginning to dawn on Margaret that the only other person, apart from herself and Ray, who knew about the wig, and who she'd deliberately kept at arm's length for all these years (she also didn't send

Christmas cards, but had neglected to mention that in the heat of the moment), that highly undesirable person was now cleaning her teeth in the luxury customer facility and perfectly capable of divulging the secret to those customers and in a single stroke ruining all Margaret's new plans. A hairdresser in a wig! A hairdresser whose own hair... she shivered. Even in the privacy of her own thoughts she didn't allow herself to remember – the memories were in a box, and the box was well and truly locked.

'So, Dilys,' she said, attempting sweetness and failing, 'how have you been all this time? How is your little girl? It was a little girl wasn't it?'

'You mean our Cheyenne,' Dilys said, 'she's following her dreams in Australia. 'Course I misses her, but the surf was calling and she had to answer. And then there's her Craig, he likes it hot. I's longing to visit her out there. Such a romantic place doncha think Marge? Palm trees and suchlike.'

Margaret had never really thought about it but she nodded and picked up a hairbrush.

'Let me tidy you up a bit,' she said, hoping to placate Dilys and distract her from mentioning hair again, 'tell you what, maybe later I can give you a trim. You want to look smart for when Steve comes to pick you up.'

At that mention of Steve, of course, Dilys burst into tears.

******

Steve had spent all Sunday evening looking for his wife and he hadn't found her. He was perfectly prepared to spend Monday evening too, and as many evenings as it took. It was quite satisfying running the highlighter over the street map showing which streets he'd checked. He'd looked in every wheelie bin, checked every alleyway, and shone his torch into every parked car, disturbing quite a few young couples. It was a sprawling town though, and he'd only covered the roads nearest to their house. He'd been thinking about it all morning at work. Standing at his bench, meticulously repairing a vacuum cleaner, he'd allowed himself the indulgence of lateral thinking. If it took one man one Sunday evening to check, um (he glanced at the map), fifteen streets, then how many evenings would it take to check... (he glanced again) rather a lot of streets? He could speed things up by driving round the streets but then of course he'd miss all the nooks and crannies. It occurred to him that he could do with some help.

So now he was spending his lunch hour with the street map and some more highlighters. Sourcing and buying the highlighters (he needed a pack with six different colours) had taken a long time, so when he got to the baker's all the sensible sandwiches (cheese, egg) were gone and he ended up with something called Chicken Tikka On Rye. It was disgusting but he barely tasted it, as the size of his task finally hit him. The town was so much bigger than he realised. He liked the fact that he could walk to work in ten minutes, and that there was a good DIY store a few minutes' drive away, but he'd forgotten just how much town there was that he never visited, including all the new housing estates on the far edges. His new idea was to divide it up into six areas and recruit five pals to help him. Or maybe six pals, that way he could coordinate their efforts. He would try to find a searcher who resided in each of the areas, thus accessing local knowledge and reducing both travel time and inconvenience.

Dilys of course was always trying to get him to go to the beach which was quite a distance from their house. He did not like the beach, he did not like sand in his shoes, or in his sandwiches, and not only did she like beach picnics but in the evenings Dilys was always keen to walk hand in hand along the sand in the moonlight. And then… the penny dropped, the lightbulb flashed. He would go to the beach after work and find her there, eating an ice cream and stroking a donkey. And his pals need never know about their marital problems.

******

Margaret had achieved near military precision with her Pensioners' Special afternoon. It wasn't her idea originally, it started when a group of five elderly friends asked her if there was a discount for bulk bookings. She put them in on a Monday afternoon, when there was never any business and most salons were closed.

Every week they turned up at two and by two thirty they were sat in a row, each with a face pack and a magazine. As the packs dried and tightened the chatter subsided and Margaret could do her work in peace, to the soothing background sound of Raymond's Golden Oldies CD. Every week they were allowed one perm and one blue rinse, with the other three having a trim, shampoo and set. They paid the same amounts each week and left at five p.m. Money for old rope.

This week though was different, what with Raymond trying to discuss tomorrow's appointment as she did her prep and Dilys demanding lunch. Eventually she had organised Ray into checking the stock room and Dilys into watching an afternoon film on TV upstairs. Her plan was to keep Dilys out of the way, get her back to Steve ASAP and hopefully forget all about her and her snide hair-based remarks after that.

Even so it was ten past two before Margaret unlocked the door of the salon. Mrs Osbiston burst past her and shuffled at top speed towards the toilet, while the other four followed more slowly but with energy to grumble. Not only had they lost ten minutes of their afternoon, but it was raining, and cold, and also too hot for Miss Stibb (who was wearing two cardigans and a woolly hat) and they were hungry and/or thirsty.

Luckily the kettle had already boiled for their complementary coffee, and they knew full well there were no complementary snacks. She'd got them more or less settled, with the face packs drying nicely, and was ready to move on to the next stage, when Raymond popped his head through the curtain.

'Margaret, um, could I see you in the stock room a moment?'

'Not now dear, I'm working.' (This was Margaret's professional voice and vocabulary. Raymond was never her dear in real life.)

'It won't take long…'

With her back to the customers she was able to give him her best icy glare, while cooing

'Could you be a love and clean these combs? I simply haven't had a chance.' Raymond gave up. He always gave up sooner or later. He took the combs and went to the small stock room where there was a sink for all salon related cleaning. Margaret pressed on with the pensioners.

She had Mrs Trundle in the chair, winding her hair onto the tiny curlers required for a tight perm, when Dilys wandered into the room. She had fallen asleep in front of the TV, the arm of the sofa had left a red pressure mark all across her face, and her hair was standing on end. There was a tomato soup stain from lunch on her hoodie and she was wearing the fluffy slippers. There was a collective gasp, and a collective cracking of the remaining face packs.

'Who's this then,' said Mrs Toogood, who had the sharpest tongue and did not live up to her name, 'Yer long lost sister? Gonna use her for a Before photo?'

Dilys blushed, but focussed on getting something to eat, and not having Ray's years of experience she didn't even notice the extra-icy glare from Margaret.

'Margaret,' she said, 'has you got any choccie bikkies?'

'Ah, poor love, she's wasting away,' said Mrs Toogood, and everyone laughed.

'They in't sisters,' offered Mrs. Osbiston, 'that's Dilys Richards that is, married to that Steve Richards.'

'What, him that's carrying on with Tanya from the chip shop?' said Mrs. Trundle. Dilys burst into tears and ran back upstairs.

******

Ray had come up with a plan to put a stop to Margaret's ridiculous daydreams. He would talk to her while they were clearing up the salon. As soon as the salon closed they always cleared up together, and made sure everything was ready for the next day. Wild horses wouldn't drag her away until the place was perfect and so she would have to listen to him while they worked. Unfortunately he didn't include Dilys in his plans and so the conversation went something like this:

Ray: so, Margaret, let's talk about…

Dilys: ohh what's this 'ere?

Ray: …tomorrow…

Margaret: it's a beauty diary. We use them for the customers to keep a record of their treatments, put it down Dilys, you'll get it all grubby.

Ray: …the solicitor…

Dilys: ooh look at these fancy hair straighteners. We never had them in my day…

Margaret: you can put them down too. Please stop fiddling with things.

Dilys: I likes hair with a bit of a curl in it meself. Remember how us used to get in our kitchen and do our hair? Me with all me curls and you poker straight? Those were the days eh Margie?

Ray: … and of course Mr. Johnson…

Margaret: ah, oh, yes, we did, erm, tell you what Dilys, how about I give you a bit of a trim right now? Or would you like a facial? Yes that's best, a nice soothing facial. Raymond can finish tidying up later.

Ray: but…

Margaret: later, Raymond.

******

LATER.

Margaret and Ray were getting ready for bed. Ray had decided to have another go at clarifying the situation re tomorrow's appointment but he was distracted by Margaret in her sleeping turban and nightdress, on her hands and knees, packing her wigs away into the bottom of the wardrobe, which was odd to say the least. It didn't occur to him that she was hiding them from Dilys.

There were four wigs. Three almost identical ones, a short style in slightly different lengths which she rotated so that it looked as if she needed a trim, and then as if she'd had a trim. The fourth wig was for parties and do's, long and glamorous and she didn't mind people knowing that it was a wig, because that was the sort of thing a hairdresser might do in a big night out. So every night there were four wigs on four wig stands lined up on her dressing table. Ray called them the Four Wigmen of the Hairpocalypse.

'Margaret…' he said to her backside, 'we need to talk.' She twisted round and looked up at him.

'She hasn't been in here has she, Ray?' she said, 'don't tell me you've let her in here?' Her eyes were full of tears and Ray was unexpectedly quite moved. After all these years together, his wife was still jealous!

'Of course not, pet,' he said, 'I told you, it wasn't like that.'

In the next room Dilys realised she was bored. She had the attention span of a flea and she was already fed up with the salon and its cramped living quarters. She decided it was time to give Steve a little nudge. So just as Ray was trying once again to talk to Margaret, there was a tap on the bedroom door. He opened it a crack.

'Ray, I needs a bedtime snack, you got any crisps in there? And can I use the phone?' Before Ray could say anything Margaret's face appeared over his shoulder.

'Dilys,' she said, 'Raymond needs his sleep. Crisps will only make your skin all greasy, and spoil the cleansing effect of your facial. Do go to bed and try to get some sleep and tomorrow we can see about, er, a makeup session for you. You'd like that wouldn't you? And you don't want shadows under your eyes when Steve sees the new you do you?'

Dilys could see the sense in this so, fighting back the tears, she trotted back to bed. And by the time Ray had been down to the bathroom and was ready to try talking again Margaret was fast asleep.

******

EVEN LATER

Steve of course did not find his wife on the beach. He found a bunch of teens enjoying cider and a bonfire, he found several couples in the shelter of various rocks and underneath the pier he found a stray dog eating a discarded burger. He would have to go with Plan B after all. So when he got home he carefully unpacked his rucksack and updated the record of places checked before sitting down with the phone. It took several rings before he got an answer from the first friend on the list. The first friend was 'busy'. The second 'friend' was also 'busy'. The third and more sensible friend asked why he hadn't told the police, since they were the professionals, the fourth call was an irate wife demanding 'do you know what time it is? We have a very early start you know.' Followed by the phone being slammed down. Steve decided to wait until tomorrow.

TUESDAY APRIL 16th

Steve woke up with the realisation that Dilys would have got all the way to Exeter before discovering that her sister was away. She didn't have a key as far as he knew, but in Phyllis's back garden was a summerhouse. Dilys loved that summerhouse, it had fairy lights and a tinkling water feature outside, with a gnome and everything (Dilys wanted one the same, but with a fairy, although there wasn't room in their tiny garden because of his shed). Obviously she would have found her way into the summerhouse and curled up on the daybed, and he happened to know that Phyllis kept her secret chocolate stash in there so she wouldn't be hungry. He would take the day off work and drive down to Exeter to fetch her home. Sorted. He phoned work, explaining he had to deal with a family emergency, and set off down the M5.

Ray woke up with the realisation that he needed backup. The solicitor would have to handle Margaret. He didn't feel guilty about palming her off, the last surviving Furkins was a grizzled old tough-as-nails solicitor who had seen it all. He was famous for being the only person ever to stop Lady Kingsford in her tracks. Furkins would cope.

Dilys woke up with the realisation that Steve was never going to turn up on the doorstep with roses and sweep her off her feet and take her home in his chariot (or Ford Fiesta). He definitely needed a nudge.

Margaret didn't wake up with any realisations. She'd done all her realising over the weekend. Now it was time for action.

Unfortunately she didn't include Dilys in her plans and so the conversation over breakfast went something like this:

Margaret: now, Raymond, we need to…

Dilys: you gonna eat that bacon rind Ray?

Ray: No. And no rush Margaret, pet, it's not till this…

Margaret: I know what time it is, Raymond, but we aren't…

Dilys: ooh lovely, ta, I likes a nice bit of crispy rind, so does Steve, maybe when you phone him you can remind him how he loves my bacon sarnies, with a droppa ketchup and…

Ray: why would I phone Steve, we ain't spoken in years…

Margaret: not now, Dilys, I need to explain things to Raymond…

Dilys: I wants him to phone Steve before he leaves for work, and tell him I's pining…

Margaret: don't be ridiculous, Dilys, let him stew, that's my advice. Raymond, I want you to move the computer down to Reception. No more using it for your silly games, we're having a proper booking system. And Dilys, don't eat that rind, you don't want greasy skin do you?'

Now Margaret turned towards Ray, determined to get her point across, but Dilys wasn't going to be deterred.

'I wants to eat it,' she said sulkily, 'and my mum always said it makes yer hair curl, worked for me dinnum?'

'Yes, yes it did,' said Margaret, backtracking hastily, 'lots of curls in your hair. We'll tidy them up a bit for Steve, later on, shall we?'

At this point of course Dilys burst into tears, and Ray thumped the table angrily, spilling ketchup all over his newspaper. Margaret treated them both to one of her icy stares and swept out.

******

It was nearly half past eight and traffic on the M5 was at a standstill. A lorry transporting toys had shed its load and the road ahead was covered in teddy bears, all with that particular vacant stare that can be so unsettling to those of a nervous disposition. Steve was a patient man and not remotely nervous. He unwrapped a humbug and sucked contentedly while embarrassed looking traffic cops with their arms full of soft toys tried to clear up.

******

Margaret had intended her dramatic sweep to reduce them both to silence but fuelled by bacon plus adrenaline, in Ray's case, and heartbreak, in Dilys's, they followed her to the salon where she was busy unlocking the door and turning the Closed sign round to Open, in anticipation of the rush that would never come.

Ray pushed past her, turned the sign back to Closed and placed his back firmly against the door. Margaret stared at him in shock, but before she could speak Dilys tapped her on the arm.

'I wants to...' she started, but Margaret silenced her with a look. Ray, seizing the chance offered by the distraction, got it all out in a rush.

'We're closed today because if you remember, Margaret, we are going to the solicitor's this very afternoon to sign the papers that will sell this salon to Mr. Johnson of the Lovely Lift chain, and then, Margaret, we're going to finish packing so we can move to the bungalow near the sea front which if you recall completes in a couple of weeks from now and we are going to start enjoying our retirement.'

'I don't think so,' said Margaret, 'I think we're going to stay put and make something of this business. All the things we've never done, or never done properly. Advertising! Special offers! Late evening opening! Hen do's! And please answer that phone, Raymond.'

He snatched it up and barked 'Yes!' And then, in a somewhat more grovelling tone, 'ah, Mr Johnson, yes, yes, all in order, yes, later this afternoon, …' Margaret grabbed the receiver from him.

'Good morning, Mr Johnson? This is Margaret Boyles, I don't believe we've met. I'm sorry to have to tell you there's been a small change of plan, a hiccup you might say, when my husband agreed to sell the salon he was not fully cognisant of my… oh, yes quite.' She fell silent for a moment, then said Goodbye and hung up, to Ray's relief.

His relief didn't last long.

'I shall be having lunch out,' Margaret said, 'I shall explain to Mr. Johnson in person. He's taking me to the Pomme D'Or, he seems a charming man, I'm sure he'll understand. Now, Dilys, since I have a little free time, how would you like a leg wax?' Ray opened his mouth to speak but she held up her hand to stop him 'you've handled this so far,' she said, 'while I slaved on, keeping the salon open. Well it's my turn now, we've arranged a day without clients so that we can see your wretched solicitor, so all you have to do is sit by the phone and take bookings while I deal with this Johnson. Now then, Dilys, legs?'

******

By late morning Steve was back home, chewing on a sandwich and making careful entries in his notebook, left hand page for Pluses and right hand page for Minuses. On the plus side, the flabby cheddar, cheap margarine and even flabbier white bread sandwich was bliss to a man who'd enjoyed every mouthful of his school dinners. And the journey home from Exeter had been without incident and very quick. On the negative side were the delay caused by the teddy bears on the way down, increasing his fuel consumption and wear and tear on the clutch, and the fact that there was no sign of Dilys in the summerhouse or anywhere else for that matter. The neighbours were quite sure she hadn't been there. This put the search for the missing wife back to square one. He put the cap back on his ballpoint pen and sat back, wondering what to do next. Perhaps the police were his best option, although he was pretty sure a grownup had to be missing for several days before they would take any notice. Really, Dilys was beyond irritating. He would have to reinstate his search.

******

Once Margaret left for her lunch date Ray felt like a condemned man. He could only think that when Margaret came home the sale would be off and there would be no money to pay for the bungalow. True,

Johnson was an affluent businessman with years of success behind him. He'd driven a very hard bargain over the sale of the salon, a bargain that Ray was yet to explain to Margaret in any detail. It was another thing he was leaving to Furkins.

But Johnson was no Furkins. And Margaret, was, well, Margaret. And she seemed to be even more Margaret since the weekend away, which had been intended to relax her and counter a recent tendency to hyperactivity, and which appeared to have had the opposite effect.

A condemned man, in Ray's opinion, deserved a pint before going to the gallows and so he was trying to persuade Dilys to look after the phone while he slipped out for some fortification. Dilys, somewhat distracted by the strange stickiness left by the leg wax and peering through spidery false eyelashes that were part of the makeup session, was having none of it.

'I hates answering phones,' she said, 'I never knows what to say.'

'It's easy,' Ray told her, 'look, I'll show you how. You pretend to be a customer phoning for an appointment, ok?'

'Ok,' she said, doubtfully, picking up the phone.

'No, no,' Ray said, 'this is pretend right? You say 'ring ring' and I'll pretend to answer.'

Dilys said 'beep beep beep' and Ray looked puzzled.

'You're engaged,' she said, 'pretend has to feel real, right?'

'Try again,' Ray said through gritted teeth. This time Dilys said 'ring ring' and Ray put his hand to his ear.

'Good morning,' he said in mellifluous tones, 'this is Aphrodite's Hair and Beauty, Mr Raymond speaking, how may I be of assistance?' Then in his normal voice 'See, it's easy, only you might have to say Good afternoon, and naturally you call yourself Miss Dilys, see what I mean?'

Dilys wasn't really listening. She had been struck by one of her better ideas. If Ray wanted her to run his business all on her own then he would have to phone Steve in return. Now he was a foreman you could phone him at work no problem, so Ray could do it right now and Steve could come for her straight away, or more likely after work. In her excitement though she gave Ray the home number.

******

Johnson picked Margaret up outside the salon in his Bentley. Something in her voice had warned him to make the extra effort, which is why he chose the Pomme d'Or, the best, or in any case the flashiest, restaurant in town.

He'd grown up in a London suburb, the very minor product of a minor public school. He didn't have it in him to compete with his peers who were all forging ahead in the City, but his grandmother died and left him a family portrait and the freehold of a retail unit in a small West Country town. It was already being run as a beauty parlour. From such a small silver spoon his entire empire was born.

He naturally felt rather superior to the West Country communities where he'd made his fortune, opening further beauty salons in small town after small town and ruthlessly disposing of the competition. He'd bought Aphrodite's purely to get rid of it, and was planning to close it down and sell it on as an empty premises.

Sure enough, the woman waiting for him outside the salon was overdressed to the nines in a very provincial way, everything far too matchy matchy. He decided she was a woman who had loved Joan Collins in *Dynasty* and had never seen a reason to update her style from then on. She, he was sure, would be just as easy to handle as her idiot husband. A deferential head waiter, a menu all in French, she'd be cowed and malleable.

He wasn't to know, because he had never bothered with local knowledge, that when Margaret was in her teens the Pomme d'Or had been the Bees Knees and it was where you went to meet boys when you were fourteen. It was all loud music and cheap perfume in those days, and you had to be sixteen to get past the doorman, which the girls could fake with mascara and hairspray and the boys got away with because the doorman was somebody's uncle and on your side. By the time you really were sixteen if you were a girl you'd added eyeshadow and high heels so that you looked old enough to get into the pubs, leaving the boys, with their pimples and squeaky voices that would never pass for eighteen, still enjoying the Bees Knees.

Margaret had met Ray in one of those pubs, down from Brum for a holiday. His Morris Minor was the only car in the car park, everyone else bumbled around on scooters. A boyfriend with a car was beyond Margaret's wildest dreams at that point, after all she reasoned, if he could afford a car he must be going places. She wasn't to know that the car had been his Nanna's, and that as far as he was concerned he'd already arrived. All he ever wanted was to live by the sea, and soon after when redundancy was offered he left his bookkeeping job in a Birmingham factory and moved to Weston.

Margaret wasn't about to be daunted by the old Bees Knees now. The head waiter was Jon Trundle, grandson of one of her Monday OAPs, but she pretended not to recognise him as he intoned 'Bong-joower madame.' As for the French menu, 'salade' with an 'e' was recognisable and all she ever allowed herself for lunch.

******

While Margaret was surveying the restaurant and wondering why none of the women present ever came to Aphrodite's (actually they were all tourists, locals weren't impressed by fake Frenchness), Ray was reluctantly phoning Steve and wondering how you start a conversation with someone you haven't seen in nearly twenty years, but in the end he said

'Steve, that you? It's Ray Boyles. Alright?'

'Well strike a light,' Steve said, 'how are you mate? Still got the Morris Minor?'

'Nah, got rid of her years ago. Sold her to a collector, still had the original paintwork, collectors like that. Margaret made me get a Rover. Only a small one mind.'

'Can't beat a Rover,' Steve said, 'solid engineering, nothing flashy.' At this point Dilys nudged Ray in the ribs and he got down to the matter in hand.

'Anyway, mate,' he said, 'it's about your Dilys.'

'Ah,' said Steve, 'she in't here right now, truth to tell, her's gone a bit missing. I just been down Exeter looking for her but...'

'Oh don't you go wasting petrol, she's right here, large as life and twice as natural, and getting herself on the outside of a Snickers bar.' Dilys blushed and whispered 'tell him I's pining.'

'Turns out she's pining, whatever that means.'

'Oh,' said Steve, 'she's keen on the old pining lark, nothing to worry about.'

'And I'm throbbing with passion for my Steve' she whispered. Ray blushed.

'And, er, throbbing apparently,' he said, 'maybe we need an ambulance.'

'Nah, never you worry, her's keen on the old throbbing too. Well, nice to hear from you mate, bye.'

Steve hung up and stared sadly at his notebook, coloured pens and street map. He'd been reluctant to start this project but now it was properly organised he was looking forward to implementing and completing it, tweaking the design along the way if necessary. Dilys was even more irritating now she was found than she had been when she was lost.

Ray put the phone down too and quickly grabbed his jacket, intent on escaping to the pub before Dilys could come up with another task for him. He'd fulfilled his side of the bargain, so for once his conscience was clear. 'If anyone calls,' he yelled over his shoulder, 'just make a note and I'll call them back.'

******

In the Pomme d'Or Johnson was sinking under the combined weight of his own smugness and gluttony. Smugness, because he had underestimated Margaret. Gluttony, because he had ordered the moules marinière and was struggling to eat them tidily, or even at all. They kept slipping out of his grasp and landing back in the broth with a splash. He simply couldn't wrestle with his food while also dealing with business. And all the time Margaret, who had barely started her salad with an e, was explaining that it had all been a dreadful misunderstanding between her husband and 'your good self' and strictly between the two of them she had to admit her husband was not the brightest sparkler in the box, but what was a girl to do, and the long and the short of it was that Aphrodite's was not for sale and there would be no signing of contracts that afternoon.

Waving away dessert, she announced that she would walk back to the salon to counteract her lovely lunch, so kind of him, and she was sure he understood.

All of which left Johnson with broth all down his chin and the fixed conviction that Margaret had played him like a fish in a bid to get more money out of him and a determination that it would never happen.

******

Dilys meanwhile was quite enjoying the solitude. She could wander unmolested round the salon, poking her nose into everything, sniffing the various creams and hair products, all of which reminded her powerfully of the time before she was married. She'd worked in the same salon as Margaret, joining as a Saturday girl when Margaret, being older, was already full time and then going full time herself as soon as she left school.

She hadn't really been cut out for hairdressing. While Margaret whizzed through the various exams Dilys loitered at the sweeping up stage, with occasional forays into washing a client's hair. She'd been far too shy for the banter that seemed to come with the job, starting usually with 'had your holidays then love?' and moving by some mysterious ritual through to mind blowing discussions about sex. She would retreat to the little room where the staff took their breaks so that no one could see her blushes. But then she realised that she did quite enjoy eavesdropping, specially when it was a bride describing her dress, which always happened before the bit where she, as it were, took the dress off. At that embarrassing point Dilys would stop listening and float away on a cloud of rose petals while she nibbled her sandwiches, and ever since she had associated food with romance.

Nostalgia was making her hungry now. Breakfast had worn off, ditto elevenses (in reality ten thirtieses and eleven thirtieses). Once she'd exhausted the possibilities of the salon she slipped into the kitchen to raid the fridge for some lunch. Soon she was settled down at the Reception desk with a plate of snacks, a cup of the complementary coffee and a copy of *Happy Ever After* magazine that Margaret took for the customers to read while they were under the dryer.

They were lovely stories, right up her street and she was completely lost in the one about a sweet natured physiotherapist and her handsome but grumpy millionaire patient when the phone rang, making her jump and swallow a peanut the wrong way. She picked up the receiver in a state of panic. What was it Ray had told her to do?

'Hello,' she said huskily, the peanut jammed somewhere in her throat, 'I'm Miss Dilys of Aphrodisiac's and I'm here to provide assistance.'

'Sorry,' said an alarmed female voice, 'I must have the wrong number. I was wanting weight loss advice, clearly you… well… you… I've got the wrong number.' She hung up and went back to doing whatever it is that the boss of a builders' merchant does. Margaret would never know how close she came to snagging the woman from the empowerment weekend as a client.

Relieved, Dilys put the phone down and coughed, which freed up the peanut. Then she remembered she was supposed to make a note of all the calls. She didn't dare write in the big appointment book but couldn't see anywhere else. In the end she ate her last aniseed twist, smoothed out the paper bag and wrote carefully 'a lady foned while I was eating me sossidge roll and peanuts she sounded a bit sad when it were the rong number.'

Perhaps, she thought, the lady was sad because she didn't have a husband who was coming to get her, sweep her off her feet and carry her home to be happier ever after. Probably. Before long though she was fretting about it. Would Steve even turn up? Maybe he'd go to the chip shop instead. She'd managed to forget about the chip shop but now all her fears came flooding back.

******

By the time Ray sailed in, fully restored to his usual bonhomie, Dilys was a nervous wreck. The phone had rung twice more, once when she was in the bathroom and once when she was deep into a story, so she had felt justified not answering it. Then she belatedly realised it was probably Steve now that he knew where she was. It was wonderful that he'd tried twice but supposing he gave up? The idea was unbearable, he had to make the first move, then she could forgive him, then they could do something romantic like share a plate of spaghetti like she'd seen in a film once. She needed advice, and Ray would have to do. But no sooner had he got his coat off than Margaret arrived, all fired up from her victory over Johnson. So much the better for Dilys, she could get two lots of advice, but she hadn't reckoned with them both being on a roll, and so the conversation went like this:

Margaret: Well, Raymond, now that's all sorted, we can get on with making something of this business. First I want you to…

Dilys: Me and Steve see, we was alright until…

Ray: What do you mean sorted? We're leaving for the solicitor's in ten minutes, that's when it will be sorted.

Dilys: I thought he'd just got a liking for their deep fried sausage but it weren't that…

Margaret: I've told him we're not selling!

Dilys: it were her, that Tanya…

Ray: what the flaming heck do you mean not selling? It's all…

Dilys: I been worried sick, weeks now I been tearing me hair out, literally, tearing it out, oh you know what I means Margie…

Margaret: aaah…

Ray: for Pete's sake, Dilys, will you let a man talk to his wife?

At which point Dilys grabbed her anorak and ran out of the salon, and Ray took one look at Margaret's white face and thought maybe he'd scored a point for once. He rammed it home by saying 'you know we'll have to pay for this solicitor's appointment whether we turn up or not, so we might as well go.' He picked up her coat, ushered her out of the door and locked the salon behind him.

******

Steve was on his way back to work. After all, the family emergency was dealt with, and he'd remembered to leave a message on Cheyenne's answerphone, so he couldn't in all honesty justify taking the afternoon off, much as he would have loved some extra time in the shed with his model railway. Then he brightened - of course, after work he could have a quick beans on toast and then spend the evening out there, painting his new stationmaster in the correct Great Western Railway livery. No need to hunt for his wife now he knew where she was.

Dilys missed the bus. She didn't want to run for it and spoil her new hairstyle, carefully shaped by Margaret to 'flatter the fuller face.' The false eyelashes still felt very odd, like a pair of butterfly wings flapping about her eyes, but Margaret had assured her she looked 'healthful and youthful'. So no running. Anyway she had plenty of time to get across town and meet Steve from work. When he saw her new look he'd forget all about that Tanya, who for a start was a fake blonde, anyone could see that, and they'd walk home hand in hand and she'd make something delicious for his tea (spaghetti so they could share it) and later she could show him her lovely smooth legs.

****

Peregrine Simpkins was quiet, shy and introverted. At school he decided that if he ever won the lottery he would move to the remotest Scottish island he could find and keep chickens. This was unlikely to happen just yet as he was too shy to be seen in a shop buying a lottery ticket but he was working up his nerve on that one. And in the meantime his parents expected him to do something with his very expensive education and so he chose the Law.

His mother had visions of him in a barrister's wig and gown, addressing a High Court judge.

However he chose to be a solicitor.

His mother then had visions of him in a smart suit in a fancy London practice, mixing in the best society - after all she reasoned, even the Royals need legal advice.

However he decided to be a country solicitor.

His mother adjusted her vision yet again so that he was wearing tweeds and providing legal assistance to, at the very least, a Duke.

He decided to apply for the smallest practice he could find, Furkins, Furkins and Furkins in the remote Somerset village of Kingsford. There was only one Furkins left, and once Peregrine arrived he rarely came into the office. Simpkins had his own visions, of quiet days behind a large wooden desk, writing the occasional will for a grateful yokel and, hopefully much later, helping the executors with probate.

Undaunted, his mother did some research and found that there was a Lady Kingsford and she had a daughter. Sixteen year old Henrietta would do very nicely for Peregrine, all he had to do was smile that sweet smile of his and Hey Presto, there would be another Mrs. Simpkins, and this one was an heiress and an Honourable.

However Henrietta was away at boarding school and Peregrine was discovering that a small country village can be a maelstrom of all the passions. Sex, anger, greed and snobbery combined together to make him a very busy man. In his first few weeks he had dealt with a feud between two village women who both laid claim to the same husband, Mrs Hetherington's long running fury which had something to do with cows and a kitchen, an argument about a valuable family heirloom, and an outraged Lady Kingsford who had been incorrectly addressed at a council meeting.

He was able to suggest to her ladyship her problem was not a legal matter but rather a lamentable social ignorance, he established that the heirloom was a fake and had no value, he stretched the truth and told Mrs Hetherington that the statute of limitations on her kitchen had expired and, in a stroke of genius, he suggested to the arguing wives that their best option was to slice the husband down the middle and take half each at which point they backed down.

He was exhausted, and glad that his rented flat was in Weston not Kingsford - there was something very suspicious about the way the village maidens seemed to constantly need to pass his office window. The office was down a medieval alley that was a dead end.

So it was with some relief he saw that there was only one appointment in his diary for Tuesday afternoon, a simple signing and witnessing of a contract that Furkins had drawn up while covering for Simpkins when he had a dental appointment, and left with Miss Dollymore the receptionist.

Ray and Margaret arrived on time, after a journey that followed their usual pattern. Margaret sat in the back of the Rover, Ray drove. Officially this was because the ride was more comfortable in the back, but in truth Margaret liked to fantasise that she was being driven by her chauffeur. Ray didn't mind, he enjoyed the silence.

Unusually though Margaret wanted to talk to him, shouting from the back seat and distracting him.

'Raymond, I've been thinking,' she yelled, 'we really need to persuade Dilys to go back home. She can't sort out her marriage at long distance, and anyway it's none of our concern.'

'Ok,' Ray said, 'whatever you want.'

'Good,' she shouted, 'I'm glad that's sorted. You can tell her when we get back.'

Miss Dollymore showed them in. At first they it seemed they were alone in the room until a cough from behind a large pile of books and papers alerted them. Peregrine had spent a long time arranging his desk as a sort of hide. He had as always rehearsed in advance what he needed to say, and he preferred to get it all out in one speech before his nerve failed. Unfortunately he hadn't been forewarned of Margaret's new mood, and so the conversation went like this:

Simpkins: I believe you are here to sign the contract for the sale of...

Margaret: we won't be signing.

Simpkins: ...your business, known for legal purposes as...

Ray: oh yes we will.

Simpkins: ...Aphrodite's Hair...

Margaret: speak for yourself, Raymond, I am not signing anything. I merely thought it was polite to explain myself in person to Mr. Furkins.

Simpkins: Simpkins

Ray: what?

Margaret: I was under the distinct impression that Mr. Furkins would deal with us personally, nothing was said about a Simpson.

Simpkins: I'm, er, Simpson, I mean Simpkins, Mr Furkins was, er, unavoidably detained.

Margaret: I see. Perhaps you would convey to Mr. Furkins my deep apologies and request him to reduce the amount owed in consideration of the fact that we have not used our full allotment of time today.

Ray: help me out here, Simpson or Simpkins, whoever you are, she has to sign, doesn't she, I mean, it's been agreed for weeks, and then there's the bungalow, I suppose old Furkins told you about that...

Simpkins: indeed, well, legally speaking Mrs. Boyles is, er, within her rights to, er, that is to say, until the document is signed and witnessed, there is no, that is to say...

Margaret: come, Raymond, we're wasting time here.

She stood to leave and Ray, beaten, followed her. Once they were in the lobby though she ducked back to the office and said

'If I were you, Mr. Simpkins or Simpson, I would look into assertiveness training. No don't thank me, it's free advice, but you could take a little something off the bill.' Assertiveness had been a key theme of the empowerment weekend. Something else Margaret had never felt the need of.

Peregrine didn't reduce the bill of course, but later on he dug out an article about assertiveness in his weekly solicitor's newsletter and very interesting it was too. And then he took the time to actually read the contract and examine the files of Aphrodite's Hair and Beauty. It was a slim file, but also very interesting.

******

Dilys caught the next bus but got off at the wrong stop, as she'd automatically headed for home. She thought of going into the house and waiting for Steve, perhaps with a rose in her teeth, but she'd somehow left her house key behind at the salon and besides he hadn't apologised yet, so she decided to stick with Plan A and meet Steve from work. She'd get him before he could even think about the chip shop, then he could apologise and then it'd be spaghetti time.

She walked back one stop and still had time to kill, so she paid a visit to the food van that was permanently parked on the edge of the industrial estate where Steve worked and that did a nice line in burgers and bacon butties. Bozza the owner always enjoyed hearing the next instalment of the Steve and Dilys saga and they passed a pleasant hour together.

Leaving Bozza to get ready for the five o' clock rush, Dilys wandered round to the gate. Sure enough, there was Steve walking across the car park, head down, hands in pockets as usual. Her heart skipped a beat and she called out to him

'Stevie, yoohoo, I's over here.'

He looked up, saw her, and his face fell. Actually fell. He wandered over. He did not offer to kiss her. Daunted, she abandoned Plan B, which was to throw herself into his arms and take his apology from that position.

'Alright, Dil?' he said, 'having a good time with Ray and Maggie?'

'I got a new look,' she said hopefully, 'Marge give me a makeover, boy you should see her now, thin as a rake, speaks like she got a mouth fulla spanners, real la-di-dah, Ray ain't changed a bit though, well he's bald as a coot mind but you knows what I mean…'

Steve looked at his watch.

'Yeah, er, thing is, Dil, I'm a bit busy this evening like, so..'

Before he could say 'so can we get on home?' Dilys burst into tears and ran away down the road. 'Busy' she knew could only mean one thing. 'Busy' was the chip shop. 'Busy' was Tanya. 'Busy' was another broken heart for Dilys. She ran. Steve was flummoxed, puzzled and confused. He went home.

******

By six thirty Steve was in his shed, painting his Victorian station master while the transistor radio kept him company with some hits of the fifties. He was determined to finish the paintwork before bedtime but he kept being distracted by thoughts of Dilys and her strange unpredictable behaviour. Why on earth would she run off like that? Why couldn't she just be normal? He was normal, most people were normal. It was infuriating and he couldn't concentrate. In the end he packed his kit away and stomped back to the house. His evening was ruined.

By six thirty Margaret was in the living room upstairs with the computer manual and a puzzled expression. She was determined to master the thing, all the other empowered women were using them, even those appalling hippies. She'd always been convinced that all machines were designed my men specifically to bamboozle women, but now she knew that it was possible to thwart their evil intentions. Somehow she would make sense of it all and as a result transform their shabby backstreet business into a roaring success.

At six-thirty Ray was in the darkened salon, brooding and sulking and wondering what to do next. He was determined to have his way for once but he was blowed if he could see how. He was afloat in a sea of bitterness and self-delusion. It's not as if I want much from life he thought (bitterly), and I've worked so hard all these years (he hadn't).

At six-thirty Dilys was walking the rain soaked streets. Her mood was sombre. She had a horrid picture in her head of Steve cosying up to Tanya and Tanya wiggling those hips of hers as she shook the chips in their basket. Somehow she found herself outside the salon and, seeing Ray's shadow, she rattled the door handle.

'I wants him back, despite everything,' she said as Ray let her in, 'and I tell you what, I'm gonna get him back. I'll do whatever it takes.'

'Well good luck to you,' Ray said glumly 'and while you're at it see if you can get my wife to sell up here and move to a lovely little bungalow with sea glimpses.'

WEDNESDAY APRIL 17th

Margaret was up with the lark and able to do an hour's computing before she opened the salon. It still wasn't making much sense. She had resolved on a leaflet drop, as recommended at the Marketing session. She could sort of see how to play around with the wording and get it just so. Then surely, she thought, she could quite cheaply print off a whole pile of leaflets. She checked her spelling and punctuation one last time.

'Are you in need of a makeover? Worried about the odd grey hair? Don't like what you see in the mirror? Come to Aphrodite's Hair and Beauty, where we can solve all your problems under one roof. Present this leaflet for our special 3 for 2 offer. (Lowest price treatment will be free if you book 3 in the same appointment)'

Triumphantly she pressed Print and the printer (which Ray had never used) whirred into action, spitting out a sheet of paper with the words in horrible faint grey type. It looked terrible, and she could see at once that it also needed colour (apricot of course, to match the business cards and the salon decor) and fancy type. And possibly a photo of a woman looking wonderful. So no printing off leaflets cheaply at home. What a waste of her time.

She felt like grinding her teeth but she'd paid a lot for her caps and she wasn't about to risk upsetting them.

Well never mind, she thought, I'll have to pop round to the print and copy shop and get them to sort something out, like they did with the business cards. I'm so close to having what I've always wanted that I can almost touch it and I'm not giving up now.

So it was a cheerful and focused Margaret who descended just before nine ready to open the salon, and she was shocked to find Ray and Dilys both slumped over the table, staring silently into their cereal bowls. She'd assumed that Dilys was back at home, but clearly she wasn't.

'Come on you two,' she said, 'Dilys, you need to start packing and Raymond, we've two trims, a leg wax and a perm this morning so…'

'I'm on strike,' Ray said, 'if I can't have what I want then I'm not doing this anymore'. And he pushed his chair back so violently that it fell over. He left the room, leaving a stunned silence behind him. Dilys recovered first.

'Oh Marge,' she said, 'I hasn't slept a wink, what's I gonna do? My Steve don't love me no more, I ain't never gonna feel his strong manly arms around me again, he ain't never gonna whisper in my ear Dilly, Dilly, don't be silly. Oh oh oh.' And she started to cry. Margaret was still staring at the door.

She had, as she'd said, a busy morning ahead, and she was used to Ray hovering in the background, inefficient and annoying but still slightly useful, sweeping up hair and so on, and answering the phone. Also she had intended for him to take Dilys home as soon as she could spare him, probably at lunch time. Instead he had abandoned her and gone swanning off simply because he had failed to understand her exciting new plans. Really the man was impossible. She eyed Dilys, who was still sniffling and using the hem of her t-shirt to wipe her nose. She was going to need some help and Dilys would have to do.

'Dilys,' she said slowly, 'never mind that now. I'll help you with the Steve problem later, I promise I will, but right now will you help me in the salon? It's only Ray's job, easy as anything, you sit at the desk, greet people, give them coffee, bring me stuff if I need it, sweep up hair and keep an eye on the ones under the dryers while I'm in the cubicle doing the leg wax.'

Dilys pushed her own chair back with a sigh and stood up.

'No, Marge, I's too shy, you knows that. Even they old ladies laughed at me cos I's fat.'

Margaret took Dilys by the shoulders and gazed into her eyes, remembering the hypnotist at the hotel.

'You,' she said, 'are a woman. You can do anything a man can do. Anything. Those old ladies are horrible like that because they never got empowerment. Trust me, you can do this.

'You really think so?' said Dilys, 'but I might have to speak to some hoity toity customer, you knows I hates all that stuff.'

'You won't have to speak to anyone,' Margaret said. She had been wondering how to keep Dilys from spilling the beans about the wig and now she had her answer. 'In fact I forbid you to speak to anyone. I'll deal with the checking in and the phone, just this once, and you can sweep up, make coffee and hand me things as I need them. Now run along and find an Aphrodite's overall in the airing cupboard. If you take that shell suit off it should fit you if you open up the adjustable tabs on the sides.'

******

If Margaret was shocked by Ray's behaviour that was nothing compared with Ray himself. He found himself out on the street walking away from the salon and waking up as if from a dream. Well he'd really gone and done it now. The look on Margaret's face!

He couldn't face going back to eat humble pie or whatever it was he'd have to do, so he mooched through the back streets, eventually arriving at the sea front, which as usual was full of older holidaymakers and trippers, mostly grey haired and clearly retired. As soon as it was the school holidays they disappeared like snow in July, to be replaced by hordes of screaming kids and exhausted parents, but in term time they were a never ending stream. A row of coaches was parked at the far end and the passengers were happily walking along the promenade despite the chilly weather, in fact a few had even hired deckchairs and were eating ice cream while wrapped up in their overcoats.

'Sorry, m'duck.' It was a woman who had bumped into him while trying to carry two plastic mugs of coffee.

'Nothing to worry about, my little sunbeam,' he said, 'no harm done.'

'Ah,' she said, 'down from Brum too are you? Nothing like a day trip to good old Weston is there?'

He smiled. He could remember feeling like that.

'Always thought we'd retire down here,' she went on, 'but we can't leave the grandkids, I expect you're the same, ooh it must be lovely to have this on the doorstep.' She indicated the windswept beach and brownish-grey waves with a nod of her head and carried on with the coffees, heading for a man who was leaning on the railings and watching the sea.

Ray remembered the first time he saw the sea at Weston. He'd driven down in his Nanna's old Morris Minor, which she gave him when she finally admitted she shouldn't be driving. He could barely afford the petrol, and he'd had to sleep in the car, but from that day on his future was decided. He would live by the sea, and he would visit it every day.

But when was the last time, he wondered now, that Margaret had let him out for long enough to enjoy the fact that they lived at the seaside. They were open on a Saturday of course, but even Sundays seemed to be filled with chores. He'd had a dream, but it hadn't worked out.

******

The Wednesday customers were nothing like the OAPs, they were younger and mostly having a break from their busy lives and so were too tired for gossip and mischief making. Two of them seem to have come with the express purpose of talking through last night's TV, the leg wax spent the whole time in the cubicle and the perm had brought a book with her to help pass the time (must be a romance Dilys thought, since the cover showed a woman in a long fancy frock embracing a man in a red uniform).

None of them seemed to notice Dilys, who went round regularly with the broom and brought the coffees, in between handing Margaret rollers and pins. Really it wasn't that different from all the years she'd spent at home, first looking after Steve's mother, a martyr to arthritis, and then bringing up Cheyenne, a late and much longed for baby who took over Dilys's life. She was still convinced that the wonderful and relaxing holiday in Majorca, despite the unpleasant event at the very end, was the reason she had finally avoided a miscarriage. Chasing round after people, seeing to their needs and keeping a smile on her face - second nature to her by now.

The morning flew by and soon Margaret was putting the snick down on the door so they could take half an hour for lunch. She found herself in something of a quandary. On the one hand, she wanted Dilys as far away as possible. On the other hand, she was going to need some help when she expanded the business. What was that old saying? Something about keeping your enemies closer than your friends?

In the back of her mind Margaret had a horrid vision of Dilys spotting someone with one of the Aphrodite leaflets that would soon be all over the town and saying cheerfully 'oh I knows her, guess what, her wears a wig!' Much better if she had a reason to keep quiet. She needed to be involved in the salon. She needed to be a, what was it called? A stakeholder, that was it. A little bit of training and she'd be a very acceptable substitute for Raymond.

******

For the rest of the day, Ray had pretended to be a tripper, reliving the heady days when Weston had seemed like a little slice of paradise. He even ate lunch in one of the overpriced tourist cafes on the sea front. He resolved that once he made it to the bungalow he would see the sea every day, even if it was just by standing on tiptoe in the attic room to catch one of those 'sea glimpses'.

It was early evening by the time he got back to the darkened salon. He let himself in quietly. He had his conciliatory speech all ready, something about stress and well, it probably didn't much matter what he said. In the gloom he could see a piece of paper on the counter with 'RAY' on it in large letters so he picked it up and headed for the stairs. He would endure the onslaught, make his peace and then come back down to the kitchen to organise the dinner.

Margaret's voice floated down, full of that hectoring over-excited tone he'd endured so much of in the last few weeks.

'But you don't understand, Dilys,' she was saying, 'this business has so much potential, all it needs is the right sort of input. Marketing! Special offers! We can give our clients a unique experience! That's what I learned at the Empowerment Weekend, we need a USP! Unique Selling Point, Dilys!'

'What, getting a haircut?' came Dilys's puzzled voice, 'nothing unique about that.'

'But you did so well today,' Margaret said, and he could tell she was getting exasperated, 'when I open my second branch I'll train you up to manage it and then that husband of yours will have to sit up and take notice. Maybe we could buy up the Kingsford salon, you'd like it there wouldn't you? The sky's the limit for empowered women, Dilys. We can do anything! We don't need men! We can do whatever we want!'

Ray turned round and tiptoed out into the street. Suddenly he couldn't face Margaret in full flood, and apparently she'd changed her mind about chucking Dilys out. He stood there for a moment, at a loss, and then it came to him. He pulled his car keys out of his pocket. He would go and see Steve. Old Steve wouldn't lecture him about profit margins and turnover. Good bloke, old Steve. Man's man.

Steve was folding his laundry, steel rule close to hand, when he heard a car pull up outside. He paid it no heed, since the large family next door were always coming and going. So it was a surprise when the doorbell rang, and even more of a surprise when he opened the door to find Ray standing there.

'Alright, mate?' he said

'All the better for seeing you,' Ray said, stepping into the hall, 'you changed that wallpaper then?'

'Yeah well Dilly kept on about it and there was a sale on so I thought why not.'

'Very nice job,' Ray said, 'lovely bit of pattern matching. You had your tea? I'm going to pick up some fish and chips.'

'Now that's a good idea,' Steve said, 'but, er, maybe best if I don't come with. If it gets back to Dil I been down there I'll be in right trouble.'

'Ah, yeah, that Tanya.'

'Yeah.'

******

Soon after Ray crept out Dilys came over all hungry so they moved down to the kitchen, where she raided the fridge and Margaret made herself a black coffee. Dilys to her delight discovered the Shepherd's Pie that Ray had intended for them to eat that evening and it was the work of a moment to microwave her share. She put grated cheese all over the top and cracked open a can of cola to have with it. Margaret watched in horrified fascination. She thought of the big boned woman at the

Empowerment weekend (who was yet to make an appointment). She thought of all the money being made by the diet industry. She thought of Mrs. Toogood's remark about a Before photo. An idea took shape.

'Dilys,' she said, 'you know I promised to help you with the Steve thing?'

'Mmmmf?' said Dilys through a mouthful of cheesy mash.

'Well you know if you lost some weight it would definitely help. If you were a little bit slimmer we could smarten you up with some new clothes and then...' Dilys swallowed the mouthful and said

'Oh no, I don't think so. My Steve likes me well-covered.'

'Really? So Tanya is plump is she?'

'Her's young yet, her ain't filled out properly.'

'And yet Steve...?' Dilys started to cry.

'It in't that, Marge,' she sobbed, 'her's got wiles, that's what's dunnit.'

'Well, you can have wiles too,' said Margaret, 'and because I made you that promise I'm going to give you a free trial of my new Diet and Beauty Makeover. We'll start with your food diary.'

'My what?'

'I'm going to give you one of my beauty diaries and I want you to write down everything about your food every day, ok?'

******

Ray soon picked up cod n chips twice, with mushy peas for him and a pickle for Steve, and very nice it was too. Tanya must have been on her night off because he was served by a man.

'Well, mate,' Steve said at last, wiping the grease from his chin, 'don't want to rush you but there's a little man in the shed who needs his buttons painting on.'

'Ah,' said Ray, 'still into the old model making then? But why not bring him in here, put a newspaper down, just the ticket on a cold evening.'

'But...' said Steve. And then it hit him. He didn't need to hide in the shed, he had peace and quiet right here in his own lounge-diner.

For the rest of the evening Steve painted, and finished, his station master, sitting at the table (with newspaper) while at the other end of the room Ray watched a video of the 1966 World Cup Final. Steve was cleaning his brush when Ray said with a sigh

'I'd better be off.'

'Alright mate. See ya.'

'Yeah, see ya.'

THURSDAY APRIL 18th

When he got back from Steve's, Ray had tiptoed in as quietly as possible, and as he'd hoped Margaret, who definitely didn't snore, was fast asleep and 'breathing heavily'. He slipped into bed very carefully and she didn't stir.

That bought him a little time before battle recommenced in the morning. He'd had had plenty of time to calm down and think, and he had his tactics ready. They'd been planning this for months hadn't they? The bungalow was all ready to go wasn't it? She'd love it once she got there, wouldn't she? She'd resisted going to Majorca and that had worked out fine, hadn't it? At least until…. possibly best not to mention Majorca.

In the morning though, as usual, Margaret caught him unawares.

'Raymond,' she said pleasantly as he came downstairs, 'could you pop to the wholesaler this morning please? I've made a list.'

'But…'

'Don't worry about the salon, I'm training Dilys up.' He now noticed that Dilys was eating a bacon sandwich and wearing a salon overall.

'But,' he said, 'we don't need supplies, we've been running them down ahead of the sale…'

Margaret ignored him and stared past him at the wall calendar.

'Of course I could arrange a delivery,' she said, to no one in particular, 'but we all know how costly that is. Dilys, don't forget to write in your notebook. Here's a pen.'

Dilys dutifully opened the book and wrote 'bacon sarnie. Cupper tea.'

'Ooh Ray,' she said, 'D'you get that note what I left you?' Ray had forgotten all about it, but he said

'Yeah sure thanks, Dil.' He sighed, picked up the list and a piece of the toast and marmalade that Dilys had made for her breakfast dessert, and headed for the door.

There was only one client booked in so most of the morning consisted of Dilys being trained to answer the phone and handle reception. Margaret had decided that if Dilys had to stick to a script for phone calls there was little chance of her saying the wrong thing. Dilys found that when things were explained clearly she could get on quite well. In fact very little had changed since her days in the Kingsford salon, and she found herself getting nostalgic. It had been fun, peeping out of the window on a Saturday afternoon looking for Steve on his moped, and fun riding home on the back of it with her arms around him and her cheek pressed against his back. A bit like a knight in shining armour he was then, but with a moped instead of a horse and a crash hat instead of a plumed helmet, and chocolate in his pocket as a treat for her. Ever since then even the smell of a hair salon made her come over all romantic (and hungry).

******

Ray actually quite enjoyed going to the wholesaler, where he was usually served by Bridie, a Brummie refugee like himself, albeit of Irish extraction. If she wasn't busy she'd give him a cup of tea and a digestive biscuit and they'd reminisce about the good old days (when you made your own amusements with a stick, ice formed on the inside of your bedroom window in winter and your dad gave you a clout round the ear if you were cheeky. Happy days.)

She could see at once that Ray wasn't his usual perky self so she gave him an extra biscuit and asked him what was up. He told her all about the sale of the salon, the pointless (begging her pardon) trip to the wholesalers, Margaret's manic behaviour, and above all the lovely little bungalow he was now committed to buying with the money he had expected from the sale of the salon.

'No more living over the flaming shop,' he told her, 'two bedrooms, proper bathroom, attic room with a little window, you can even see the sea from up there, I've been calling it Margaret's boudoir but now she refuses to live there. I don't know what I'm going to do, Bridie.'

'For a start you're going to drink that tea, and you're going to take your supplies on sale or return for when she comes to her senses. Ooh, tell you what, if she wants to keep working, why not set her up as a mobile hairdresser? She won't need the salon then, she can work when it suits her. Get her one of those mobile phones, clients can phone her direct, a nice little bag for all her kit, Bob's your uncle.'

'That is one brilliant idea,' Ray said, 'I'll go straight back and tell her.'

'Finish your order first,' said Bridie, nodding at the second piece of paper that had come out of Ray's pocket. He picked it up. It was the note from Dilys.

"RAY" it read *"Mr Simpkinson foned about something called interestin News maybe you is gonna be in the papers?"*

'Bridie,' Ray said, 'could you be an absolute poppet and let me use your phone?'

******

Steve was so excited at work all day he could barely concentrate. He was bursting with ideas for changing things around, bringing all his bits and pieces in from the shed and really getting to grips with the various buildings his model railway layout needed. It was so much easier to work inside where there was plenty of room. Everything was going to be ok!

After phoning Furkins, Furkins and Furkins and also in a state of high excitement Ray jumped in the car, drove to Kingsford, saw Simpkins, was very interested indeed in the interesting news, and then he went straight into the town centre and found a mobile phone retailer. The price of the things was unbelievable but he didn't care, because it was worth it to persuade Margaret to move. Everything was going to be ok!

Dilys also found herself getting excited about being a salon manageress. It really wasn't as difficult as all that, as Margaret said to her all those years of running round after Steve and Steve's mum and Cheyenne had given her, what was it? Excellent something, and organisational skills, whatever they were, and empowermenting. Never mind what it was called, she would soon be slim and beautiful with a proper job, one where you didn't come home stinking of fish and cooking oil like that Tanya, and Steve would be so bowled over he would beg her to come home. Everything was going to be ok!

Margaret was too busy to be excited. Taking the salon upmarket and opening a second branch required a lot of planning and careful thought. Everything was already ok.

She came downstairs after another long session wrestling with the computer, trying to persuade it to create her five year business plan, having left Dilys to mind the shop while it was quiet. She found her sitting at the Reception desk eating a chocolate bar.

'Dilys,' she said, 'we don't eat in the salon. We eat in the staff facilities out of sight of the customers, and we wipe the chocolate off our chops before we return to our post in the salon. Now, since you're moving on to Reception you won't be wearing an overall, you'll be smartly dressed as the public face of Aphrodite's, and you certainly won't want crumbs all down your front. And don't forget to put that chocolate bar in your notebook.'

Dilys obediently picked up the pen and when she had finished writing Margaret took the notebook from her and flicked through it. There were an astonishing number of items, listed haphazardly in an apparently random order:

"Cheese sarnie, toffee apple, hang on there were some pikkel innit, bitta cake, canna coke, cuppa tea with that sarnie, 3 aniseed twists, cornflakes, 2 more twists, peanuts..."

'Dilys,' she said, 'it's a wonder you don't burst. Why on earth do you eat so much? You can't be hungry.'

'I dunno,' said Dilys, 'it cheers me up dunnit, and it tastes nice. Food's good for you mind, they told us that in school, remember that woman in the overall, come in Wednesday afternoons and done cooking with us?'

'Never mind the nostalgia trip,' Margaret said, 'we can't work with this, it makes no sense. Look, do it like this. Put the name of the meal, right, Breakfast, Lunch, Dinner, or Snack. Then underneath put the time. Underneath that put what you ate and then, Dilys this is really important, write down what you were thinking. Like a diary, OK, but for food. Then we can go through it and work out what's going on for you and the best way for you to cut down a bit.' Or cut down a lot, she thought, but didn't say. Baby steps. And no triggering her into making sly hair based remarks.

Just at that minute Ray walked through the door, beaming from ear to ear. He ran up to Margaret and hugged her before she could stop him.

'Everything is sorted,' he said, 'everything is gonna be OK. Here, this is for you.' He thrust the box at her. She looked at the label.

'Thank you, Raymond,' she said, 'but I don't need a mobile phone, we have a perfectly good phone here in the salon.'

'We've sold the salon,' Ray gabbled, 'but don't you fret, you'll love your new mobile hairdressing business, get you out of the house, sorry, bungalow, bit of pin money, that'll come in handy, money's going to be tight so...' He ground to a halt. He'd seen his wife's face.

'Mobile hairdressing,' she hissed, 'you expect me to trudge round carrying all my equipment and supplies and work in people's kitchens? In between the cat's litter tray and some liver frying on the stove I suppose?'

'You'd have the car,' he said weakly, 'you wouldn't have to trudge.'

'What about me?' Dilys said, 'I'm susposed to be managing the new branch.' They both ignored her. Margaret pushed the box at Ray.

'Take it back,' she said, 'get a refund on the stupid thing. Now if you'll excuse me, I have a salon to run.'

'No point,' Ray said, 'I told you, I sold it. Went over there this afternoon and signed. It's done Margaret, and it can't be undone.' Margaret fixed him with a glare that would freeze hell.

'I,' she said, 'have not signed anything.'

'Blimey, Ray,' said Dilys, ' did you forge her signature? You can go to prison for forgery you know.' Ray hadn't taken his eyes off Margaret, as if she were a Rottweiler which might pounce at any moment.

'I didn't have to forge anything,' he said, desperately trying to keep his voice from shaking, 'Simpkins noticed it was all in my name. Remember, that the time the accountant said it'd be a good idea?'

Margaret could barely speak but she gasped out something that sounded like 'temporary'.

'Oh yes,' said Ray, now affecting a nonchalance he was far from feeling, 'meant to be temporary just for that tax year but somehow it never got changed back. So I signed. It's done.'

A ghastly silence fell. With great dignity Margaret turned and headed for the stairs. Then she stopped.

'Don't you think I'll be moving to that bungalow,' she said, 'I haven't signed for that have I.'

'Yes you have,' Ray said, puzzled, 'weeks ago, we went over there and got everything signed ready for exchange. You must remember, afterwards I dropped you at the surgery so you could see the doc. You weren't feeling great but you definitely signed.' There was an even ghastlier silence.

'I,' said Margaret at last, with a calm that she was far from feeling, 'will be sleeping alone tonight.' And she swept up the stairs, nose in the air. Then they heard the slam of the bedroom door. Dilys and Ray looked at each other.

'S'ok,' Dilys said, 'you have my room. It's time I was getting back to my own bed anyway.'

******

Seeing Ray and Margaret like that had made Dilys realise that she was being foolish, holding out for an apology from Steve and worrying about that Tanya. What did anniversaries and Tanyas matter when it came down to it? Her Steve would never go selling her salon and buying her mobile phones what she didn't even want. Sitting on the bus she could feel herself welling up. She couldn't wait to get home and tell Steve he was forgiven. She was a new woman now, well maybe she hadn't quite lost any weight yet or bought any new clothes or started managing a salon but inside she was already a different Dilys.

Then she had an even better idea. She could feel the empowermenting surging through her veins. It was the perfect time to get off the bus one stop later and go and give that Tanya a piece of her mind.

Sure enough, there she was, wiping down the counter and singing along to the radio like she wasn't even interested in stealing other people's husbands.

'Hello,' she said, bold as brass, 'what can I get yer?'

'I'll tell yer what you can get me,' Dilys said, 'with yer hips and yer wiles, well no more of it, d'you hear me?'

'I'm sorry, chips and what?' Tanya said, reaching to turn down the radio, but it was too late, Dilys had turned and swept out, copying Margaret, leaving Tanya with the order pad in her hand and her mouth hanging open. The owner stuck his head out from behind the fryer.

'Don't let it bother you love,' he said, 'it's only Dilys from down the road, world of her own that one. You done with that counter yet?'

Dilys was still on a high as she strode up the garden path. I'm a woman, she thought, I can do anything. She tripped on the step and dropped her key so she rang the bell and as she straightened from picking up the key there was Steve opening the door just in time for her to fall into his arms.

Steve didn't want a repeat of the running away episode outside work so he quickly pulled her into the hallway and closed the door. This is more like it, Dilys thought, any minute now I can forgive him and tell him to forget all about Tanya 'cos I've sorted that one out and no mistake. There was barely room for the two of them, the tiny hall was piled high with cardboard boxes. Dilys was about to speak, then she saw the label on the nearest one. It read 'candles' in Steve's neat writing. The next one said 'China bits'. She looked at Steve, puzzled.

'It's alright,' he said, 'I wrapped 'em up nice, gonna put 'em in the loft, nice and safe like.'

Dilys pushed past him into the lounge-diner. She could hardly believe her eyes. The sofa was covered in a shiny black tarpaulin and neatly laid out along it were Steve's locomotives and carriages. The table was covered in newspaper, as was the floor, and on the table was another loco in bits. Her display shelves were also newspapered and held, not her candles and China ornaments, but tiny paint pots and brushes. She turned and went into the kitchen. It was very tidy, apart from the pile of balsa wood on the drainer. There was a saucepan, plate, mug, knife and fork neatly laid out, with a tin of beans and a loaf of bread.

Dilys surveyed the wreck of her home.

'Oh, Steve,' she said, 'how could you?'

'You weren't even here,' he said indignantly. The new empowered Dilys wasn't having any of that, and she was fresh from a lesson on wounded dignity from Margaret.

'I,' she said, 'am gonna sleep in my own bed tonight.' She saw Steve's puzzled look. 'You can have Cheyenne's room,' she explained. She turned to the stairs ready to sweep impressively up them, but then she remembered something.

'But first I'm gonna have a bitta toast.'

'Fair enough,' said Steve, 'make me some while you're at it will you?

FRIDAY APRIL 19th

Ray was awake all night. He was beginning to think he may have gone just a tad too far. But it was done, and couldn't be undone. The problem was, it was him what done it, and him what would suffer for it. So I've sold the salon, he thought, so she'll have to move to the bungalow. She's bound to see sense sooner or later. Isn't she?

He was pretty sure Margaret was awake, since he couldn't hear her breathing aka heavy breathing aka snoring.

In the room next door Margaret *was* awake. She was trying to work out what to do. So he's sold my salon, she thought, well it's not the only salon in the world, I'll get another one. How hard can it be? I'll need somewhere to live too, I'm not living in that poky little apology for a house. I'll draw up that business plan then I can get a bank loan. What else. Oh yes Dilys, she can work for me, and when she loses some weight we'll start that weight loss advice side line. I did it on my own but if some women need a helping hand well so be it.

Dilys was awake too. The bed was awful big and awful cold without Steve. Something had gotten into him for sure, lots of times she'd gone for a few days and he was always so pleased to have her back. Not this time, this time he was too busy wrecking their lovely home. All her candles and knickknacks, every single one of them precious and meaningful, shoved into cardboard boxes. It must be that Tanya. She was the home wrecker.

Steve was asleep, the deep and restful sleep of the man who has no idea what he has done.

Now Dilys was running through her bits and pieces in her head. Her china fishing dog, with a bit of wire for a fishing line, that she bought in Woolacombe on their first whole day out together, that she carried all the way home on the back of his scooter. The brass Dutch girl with a bell inside her skirt that came from Nan's house after she died. The swan sailing along on a mirror that she got from Santa in Woolies when she was fourteen. And above all her Charles and Di souvenir mug, the symbol of true love and happy ever after and never mind what it said about them on the news. In the end she gave up on sleep and crept downstairs and put the living room to rights. She unpacked her boxes. She put all the newspaper in a bin liner, all the loco bits in a takeaway box and all the rest of the modelling stuff in the storage boxes. She crossed out Steve's labelling and wrote 'Steve's Toys' in her chaotic scrawl and shoved it all out into the hall. Then she carefully replaced all her things and made the room nice again. She put her Charles and Di wedding mug in her bag, deciding that in future it would go everywhere with her. After that, feeling better, she closed the door, went back to bed and dozed fitfully for a few hours. In the morning though she found herself making Steve's sandwiches on autopilot. He grabbed them from her, said 'bye bye Dil' and left. He didn't even notice the changes to the cardboard boxes in the hall, as usual he was in a rush to be out by 7.45 to be at work for 7.55 ready to start at eight on the dot.

Once he had left Dilys went into their bedroom determined to find something smart to wear for her new life as Manageress of a salon. Even though Ray had sold it she had absolute faith that Margaret would get it back. After all, she remembered Margaret from school, standing up to teachers who punished her for not having the correct uniform. Her parents couldn't afford it, but instead of admitting to that Margaret pretended to be a defiant rebel and sat in detention day after day until the teachers gave up.

She rummaged through her wardrobe. Not a shell suit. Not trackie bottoms. Not trainers. Definitely not slippers. At the back of the wardrobe she found the plain black dress she'd bought for the funeral of poor old Jock from down the road. She barely knew him till his wife died, and then he was a lost soul always grateful for someone to chat to, and then a few months later he was gone. They said cancer but she knew better, she knew a broken heart when she saw one.

The dress still fitted, except the zip at the side wouldn't do up. The only tights she could find were some green glittery ones that Cheyenne wore one Christmas. 'One size fits all' - just about. They looked a bit odd but she had some knee length black boots that covered them up, they gave her gyp but you had to suffer to be beautiful didn't you. Then she had a brainwave about the zip, she still had the pink brocade jacket she bought for Cheyenne's wedding, never worn because the little minx swanned off to Australia with Craig without so much as bothering to get married. It fitted her as long as she didn't try to do up the buttons and it would hide the bit at the side of the dress where her flesh bulged out through the zipper opening.

Pausing only to grab a peanut butter and jam sandwich she headed for the bus stop. Margaret would be surprised to see her so early and so smart.

Margaret was surprised, and even a bit pleased.

'Oh, Dilys,' she said, 'you have made an effort. And just when I need you too. If you could hold the fort for a couple of hours, I need to run out. I know it's Friday but fortunately we're very quiet this morning and I'll be back in time for the trim at 11.30. Here's a hanger for your jacket.'

'Oh you're alright,' Dilys said awkwardly, 'I'll keep it on for now.' Margaret gave her a funny look but didn't say anything.

'All you have to do is answer the phone,' Margaret said, 'remember what I told you to say? No chatting with the callers remember? Be professional, stick to the script. And if Raymond emerges from his pit don't tell him what I'm doing will you?'

'Alright. What are you doing then?'

'Better you don't know.' And she was gone.

Margaret's first port of call was Simpkins. It was ten to nine but he was already at work, ploughing through the chaos of documents that Furkins had dumped on his desk. She was pleased to see his barricade of books was considerably smaller, but he still had the startled look of a baby bird that's fallen out of the nest.

'Mr. Simpkins,' she said, 'I need you to explain to me how I have somehow sold my salon and bought a bungalow without wanting to do either.'

Simpkins launched into a complicated legal explanation that she couldn't really follow, not that she was going to let him know that, but it ended with

'So you see, dear lady, while the two transactions are not connected in any legal sense they are undoubtedly both complete down to the last detail. You have indeed sold your salon, and you have bought your bungalow with the proceeds thereof, and may I be so bold as to wish you a very happy retirement.'

Margaret did not mind being his Dear Lady, in fact she was pleased to hear him sounding much more like a proper solicitor, although she wasn't going to let him know that either.

'You may not,' she said, 'you may brace yourself for assisting me with the purchase or possibly lease of my new salon and the rental or possibly purchase of my new residential property. But first please confirm that I have possession of my salon for another six weeks?' Simpkins glanced at the calendar.

'Indeed,' he said, 'but you…' Margaret stood up .

'Six weeks will be ample for my purposes,' she said, opening the door, 'and that gives you time to call in at my current salon for a trim. A decent haircut will give you what I believe is called gravitas, always useful to someone in the legal profession. Good morning.

******

Sure enough, once Margaret had disappeared Ray crept in, still in his dressing gown. He found Dilys at the Reception desk, scribbling away in a notebook.

'What you up to, pet?' he said, 'don't tell me we've had a flurry of phone calls.'

'No silly,' she said, 'it's me food diary innit. I've gotta write down everything what I eats and what I's thinking of and how I's feeling so I can get thinner and then Steve won't want that Tanya anymore.'

'I'm pretty sure you'll have to cut down on sweets and stuff too,' Ray told her, nodding at the bag of liquorice allsorts on the desk, 'writing it down isn't a magic fix you know, And don't let Margaret catch you with food in the salon.' Dilys stuck her nose in the air. That wasn't any way to talk to a potential Manageress.

'Margaret and me...' she started

'Where is she anyway? What's she up to?'

'I in't gonna tell ya.'

'Oh come on pet, I thought we were pals. Didn't I take you in…'

'Ooh yes you did, took me in to the bosom of your family in my hour of need when my heart was broken.'

'Well then, where's she gone?'

'I dunno. Her wouldn't tell me. But if I was you I'd get dressed before she gets back.'

******

Margaret's second stop was at the bank where she asked to see the Manager. He was middle aged and fleshy, he looked rather like the cuckoo that had pushed Simpkins out of the nest. When she explained that she wanted a loan, he said she needed an appointment with the Loans Manager, looked at his watch and stood up to show her out. Margaret ignored this, focussing on a spot somewhere over his right shoulder, and started explaining what a good investment her new business would be, and how many long term loyal clients she had, including, funnily enough, the Manager's cleaning lady, and what a chatterbox she was! At that point the manager turned pale, sat down with a thump and said to leave it with him and he'd see what he could do.

Finally Margaret ran in to see Barbara. Barbara was a unique combination of customer and friend plus a source of local news/gossip. Her husband was often away working and she enjoyed a life of leisure in their penthouse flat on the seafront. She'd just returned from a holiday so there was a lot of catching up to do. Of course she wanted to know all about Margaret's spa weekend, and was astonished when she heard that it was no such thing, and even more astonished when she heard that Ray had sold the salon from under her ('But don't you worry,' Margaret said, 'I'm going to have another one, all my own and bigger and better than Aphrodite's').

It was another black mark against Ray - Margaret often used both Ray and the salon as excuses when Barbara suggested anything awkward, such as swimming at her club, or going to their timeshare in Spain as a foursome. Barbara of course knew nothing about the wigs.

'And he thinks I'm going to live in that bungalow!' Margaret continued, 'wild horses wouldn't drag me to it let me tell you.' She could feel the prickle of tears on their way, and knew she had to get out of there before she broke down. The rest of the news could wait till later - Barbara didn't know Steve and Dilys anyway, she probably didn't even know there was a council estate on the edge of town.

'Anyway, darling,' she said quickly, 'I must dash, the salon calls. See you Sunday?'

'Ah, no, we're driving up to his mother's,' Barbara said, 'dreadful bore and we'll be late back, you know what the traffic's like on a Sunday. Anyway I'll see you out, I really must tell you what my neighbour told me. You know, the one that works at the estate agent's?' She carried on talking as she saw Margaret to the car. It was very interesting news. Very interesting indeed.

All in all a most satisfying morning's work, and she was back in plenty of time for her customer. And there was Ray, (dressed) distracting Dilys, who was eating, as per usual. Really people were too annoying.

'Ah, Margaret,' Ray said, 'I was wondering, er, that is, have you had a good morning? Is there anything you want me to do?'

Truly the man was an idiot. He had a list of unfinished, nay unstarted, jobs, as long as his arm, but would it ever occur to him to get on with any of them ? No it would not.

'I do believe, Raymond,' she said, 'that you have retired. Dilys and I can manage perfectly well without you. Run along and do whatever it is that old men do all day.'

******

Ray grabbed his jacket and left before she changed her mind. Without really thinking he ambled along to the sea front again. The tide was in and he sucked in a deep refreshing breath. Ahh, he thought, isn't that just the ticket. He watched the waves for a while and then on a whim he walked round to the bungalow. Only ten minutes from the sea and in a couple of weeks it would be his! He saw himself with a dog, a cheeky little mongrel, mooching to the sea front every morning, coming back with the paper to his perfect little home.

The neat front garden (ok, it needed tidying and the grass was knee high but in his imagination it was neat, and all without him having to lift a finger). The red front door between the two front bay windows (again, the door was brown but in his mind he or somebody cheap had already painted it a cheerful red). Above all the Estate Agents' board, leaning at a slight angle and with SOLD across it. Ray smiled happily and headed for his new local at the end of the road, the fantasy dog trotting beside him. He'd promised to stay on the darts team for his old local near the salon, but the new one looked promising, and a man can't have too many locals after all. The new one had an interesting reputation for homemade pies, and today would be the perfect chance to give one a try.

He knew the pub was alright, he'd been there once or twice for skittles but never for food. Now he learned it served a decent pint, two friendly old blokes were playing dominoes in the corner, and the pie was delicious.

It was also eye wateringly expensive. Ray's happy mood evaporated like snow on a hot tin roof. How on earth was he going to afford all this? He'd worked it out to the nearest penny and with Margaret jumping ship it hit him that he could be in real trouble re money. Regretfully he cancelled the dog, and still found himself unable to pay for his new life.

******

Margaret dealt with the trim, sold the client some face cream and settled down in the back room to check Dilys's notebook.

'Dilys,' she said after a few minutes, 'your spelling is atrocious. As for your grammar, it's perfectly shameful.'

'Oh don't go on at I, Marge,' Dilys said, 'you knows I struggles. I's probably got that dislocatial thing, Sindy down the road's little boy's got it, 'course nowadays they give you special help at school but we never had none of that did we, we was too poor for all that.'

'It's pure laziness, Dilys, and you know it. They tried hard enough with us at school, but you didn't bother. You don't hear me speaking like that do you? And may I remind you we grew up on the same street and at least your father had a job.'

'Ooh that in't fair, I did try. I used to get in a right old state over that homework what they was always giving us. Don't be mean to I, Marge.'

But Margaret was on a roll, and as ever she found it hard to stop. She forgot all about keeping Dilys sweet.

'It says here "ten past ten I had one of they Peppermint Aeros what Steve used to buy me when we was courtin, right romantical he was in them days." For a start, Dilys, there's no such word as romantical.' (She was wrong, but then she too had left school at sixteen).

'I in't clever like you,' Dilys said sulkily, 'Every Sunday night I'd be sat at home trying to do me homework and tearing me hair out, literally, tearing me hair right out!' And she grabbed her curls with both hands and gave them a good tug, by way of illustration.

Margaret gasped and her hand flew involuntarily to her wig. There it was again, the minute you said anything, there was that sly dig about hair, letting you know that she knew!

Time to backtrack. She took a deep breath and did an about-face.

'Never mind,' she said, 'you're going to be my manageress, it's not like you'll be writing books is it. I need excellent customer service skills and administrative efficiency from you, I'm sure you can cope with those, Dilys, we won't worry about your spelling.'

Just at that moment the shop bell pinged, giving them a good excuse to abandon the upsetting conversation. It was Simpkins, looking sheepish and hesitant.

'Why Mr. Simpkins, how good of you to come,' Margaret said.

'Yes,' he said, 'the thing is…'

'Dilys, do get Mr. Simpkins a robe, we use the blue ones for our gentlemen, and a hot towel of course, so soothing for the face, while I tidy up his hair. Do sit here Mr Simpkins, now please relax and forget all about your cares at Furkins, Furkins and Furkins for a few precious minutes.'

'Ooh,' said Dilys, returning with the robe and the towel, 'young Dolly work for you dinnum? Lovely girl, used to play with our Cheyenne after school while her was waiting for the bus back to Kingsford.'

'Murrfe' said poor Simpkins, now wrapped like a mummy and quite unable to find the nerve to deliver the important information he had for Margaret.

'You knows, Marge, er, Mrs Boyles,' Dilys went on, 'Beryl Dollymore's girl, didn't want to work on the farm like her brothers. Can't say as I blames her, what with all them chickens, and turkeys too at Christmas, coo I wish I could get my Steve to eat turkey but he won't, his mum tried one time, told him it were chicken but he weren't fooled, oh no, not Steve…'

'Dilys,' Margaret said, 'could you be a love and, er, tidy the stock room for me? Thank you so much.'

Twenty minutes later Simpkins, feeling rather naked around the ears and pink around the cheeks, and clutching a bottle of Men's Skin Moisturiser, was on his way back to Kingsford without having found a way to tell Margaret his news. He was beginning to sound like a solicitor, and look like a solicitor, but he still didn't act like a solicitor.

******

Ray had his calculator in his pocket and he sat on the front garden wall with it. Somehow he had to make the figures add up.

They didn't. Crunch them whichever way he did, there wasn't going to be anything to live on if he retired and moved without Margaret's contribution. And if he sold the bungalow, they'd be homeless. And if Margaret wasn't moving, where would she live? Really the only option was for Margaret to see sense and stick with the plan.

Having decided that she would simply have to, he stopped worrying about it and decided to swing by Steve's work and catch him in the lunch hour. He was realising how much he'd missed old Steve, fair enough he could be a bit of a stick in the mud, bit set in his ways, also inclined to bang on about DIY and toy trains, but even so he was a diamond geezer. In fact he'd never quite understood why the friendship had been allowed to lapse. He had a vague memory of Margaret insisting on No Visitors when they got back from Majorca and she was in the hospital, but after that it was all a blur.

'Alright?' Steve said, seeing his friend waiting in the car park, 'want one of me cheese sarnies?'

'Nah you're alright, I had lunch in the pub,' Ray said, 'but I could do with a coffee.' So they strolled across to Bozza's van and perched on the fence to eat and drink.

'How's Dil?' Steve said, 'alright is she? Her's a funny one and no mistake.'

'Ah,' said Ray, 'she's got it into her head that you're carrying on with that Tanya.'

Steve sighed.

'I know,' he said, 'I'll be honest with you, it seemed like a good idea at the time, you know, buy me a bit of peace and quiet like, never crossed my mind she'd go this ballistic though.'

'We'll it's fair enough, mate, it might seem like a bit of harmless hanky panky to you but girls are sensitive to that sort of thing.'

'Hanky panky! I'm not like that, you know I'm not. Truth is I was only mending the girl's sunglasses, seen her outside Tesco looking upset, little screwdriver on me penknife see?' He pulled the penknife out and showed Ray its many attachments.

'Nice,' said Ray, 'I like the little magnifying glass, very neat.'

'Yes,' said Steve, 'it cost us a bit but it was well worth it, I tightened up the screw for her in no time. Course some old biddy saw us stood there together. Tells Dil. Dil gets upset. And then no more romance.

Lovely it were. Peaceful. So like I say, seemed like a good idea to let her run with it for a bit.'

'Now that I can understand.'

'No more "ooh Steve give I a kiss" just when you've got to the fiddly bit on a model assembly, no more "ooh Steve, let's have candles at tea time."'

'Candles! Can't see what you're eating! Nasty things, candles.'

They were both silent for a moment, remembering. Then Steve had an idea.

'I been thinking,' he said, 'how about you come up Brissle with me tomorrow. I gotta get some stuff for me modelling and I hates driving round the city. Second nature for you Brummies though.'

'Happy to oblige,' Ray said, and then, embarrassed, 'but I'll be asking you to put something in the kitty for petrol. The finances are all over the shop now Margaret's let me down over the bungalow. I can't get her to see sense.'

'Ah, she always was a feisty one. Coo you should have seen her back in the day, I remember in the Infants the school bully had a go at her, big boy, but soft like, and he only picked on the girls. Well she had this, whaderyercallit, a duffle bag, that's it. She swung it by the handle and caught him smack in the face, full on. Knocked him sideways. Reckon he was seeing stars for a week. She wouldn't let no one touch Dil neither, seeing as they lived on the same street and walked in together.' Steve's brain conveniently did not supply him with a memory of Margaret a few years later when that feistiness turned on him, instead he floated comfortably in a rose-tinted cloud of nostalgia.

'She's mellowed a bit since then but she's still pretty tough,' Ray said, 'even so I can't get over how she's changed these last few weeks. She was happy enough about selling up, I'm sure she was, and now she won't play ball at all. It's a mystery, that's what it is mate, a right flaming mystery.'

******

When Dilys got home that evening, having stopped off at the pizza place on the way because she'd decided Steve didn't deserve her cooking, she was annoyed to find he was already in the shed, and his tea of, yes, beans on toast, had already been consumed, washed up and tidied away. So she watched her bootleg video of *Four Weddings* for the umpteenth time and went to bed early. On the bedroom door she stuck a large piece of paper with NO! written on it and an arrow pointing to Cheyenne's room. So yet again Steve slept contentedly in his daughter's nest of cuddly toys.

******

    Ray on the other hand, also banished to the spare room, hardly slept at all. The row with Margaret had been spectacular. Ray was a peaceable man, not to say a lazy one, so he rarely bothered with rows, but he'd been feeling desperate. He'd reminded Margaret of their plan to both take their occupational pensions early so that they could afford the living costs of the bungalow. She refused, saying that was one thing she would never sign, and went on to demand half the proceeds of the salon sale to help finance her new business. Ray reminded her they'd bought the salon with his redundancy. She explained to him it was her skill that had kept it going all these years. He told her he had kept the books perfectly, both the accountant and the tax man were happy and that must count for something. She said it was his one contribution, he'd never even finished his book keeping qualification and anyway she could do books perfectly well herself. Ray said he couldn't afford to live in the bungalow. She yelled 'so get a lodger' and stormed off to bed, slamming the door. He didn't need a notice to tell him to sleep in the spare room.

SATURDAY APRIL 20th

Fridays and Saturdays are always the busiest days in a hair and beauty salon. At Aphrodite's things would usually start slowly on Friday morning, with a few stay-at-home older women who had the time, money and inclination to get themselves tarted up for the weekend. Ladies of leisure were a dying breed and Ray called them The Last of the Oldhicans. Then there would be a busy lunchtime with girls who worked locally rushing in for a quick beautify followed by an afternoon and evening of women who'd left work early or dashed in after work because they had something special at the weekend.

Saturdays were nonstop, usually teens planning a big night out on a tight budget - Aphrodite's was famously cheap. On good Saturdays Margaret had a facial relaxing in the cubicle, a hair dye and/or highlights curing, ditto a perm, a blow dry in hand and a row of customers waiting their turn. The old fashioned dryers were rarely used on a Saturday and very few men risked it, in fact very few men risked it on any day of the week despite the hot towels and fetching blue cover ups.

It was these two days that kept the salon solvent, but only just. Recently though it had been quieter, and they had struggled on for a while without Saturday girls (partly due to a distinct lack of local teenagers who could cope with Margaret's demands). Ray would be obliged to work quite hard for those two days, with no time at all for the sports pages of the newspaper. Margaret called it his Two Day Week.

But now he was on a No Day Week. Margaret found she could get just as much done with Dilys helping, and Dilys already knew that she lost none of her old hair sweeping skills. Even better, she wasn't as shy as the young Dilys. Back then the customers either reminded her of her mum, known locally as 'that there old battleaxe at number 53', or they were young and pretty and made Dilys feel like a lump (although she had good hair. No one could deny she had thick curly naturally blonde hair.) But time had passed and now she found that the young ones reminded her of Cheyenne and she felt motherly towards them. She did compare herself unfavourably with the older ones sometimes but on the whole she was too busy to think about it. A couple of them even tipped her, and Margaret showed her the tip box, which would be shared out on an equitable basis, whatever that was.

******

The moment Steve jumped in the car (front seat of course, none of that back seat nonsense) he turned the radio on. It was already tuned to Ray's favourite nostalgia based station and they settled back happily to the music of their youth. Apart from briefly telling Ray roughly where they were headed, he didn't speak again till the last few minutes, when he took out a street map so he could give final directions to the model railway shop. Very restful thought Ray, very pleasant to tootle along without anyone complaining about my speed or asking for the heater on.

The shop was in a suburb, a sprawling non-descript area developed in the 1930's. They had to park in a side street but it was only a short walk to the model shop, part of a dilapidated row of shops that included a wool shop, a paper shop, a bookies and inevitably, a hairdressers.

'Coming in?' Steve said, pulling a list out of his pocket.

'If it's all the same to you I'll give it a miss,' Ray said, 'I'll pick up a paper and sit on that bench over there.'

'Fair enough,' Steve said, 'but if I'm not out in an hour come and get me, I can lose all sense of time in there. Like an Aladdin's cave it is.'

In fact he was out in forty-five minutes, with two carrier bags full of cardboard boxes that he stowed carefully in the boot.

'Phew,' he said, 'that's broke the bank and no mistake. Good job you brought the lunch mate.'

They took themselves off to a park to eat it, and were rewarded with spectacular views across Bristol. Expecting a cheese and pickle sandwich at best, Steve was astonished to open his box and find a slice of homemade cold chicken pie nestling on a bed of lettuce with some cold new potatoes and a separate little pot of cole slaw.

'It's only cabbage and carrot,' Ray said, 'but I wasn't sure if it was your cup of tea. Made the pie earlier in the week, but I always do a big one so there's plenty of left overs. Not that we get many leftovers since your Dilys turned up. I had to put a label on this one to warn her off it.'

'Blimey,' Steve said, pushing the pot of cole slaw to one side, 'didn't know you was a chef like. Didn't know you could cook.'

'Had to learn didn't I,' Ray said, 'Margaret was never gonna bother. It's easy once you get the hang of it.' Remembering his own kitchen disasters Steve was impressed. He didn't know, or maybe had forgotten, that 'getting the hang of it' was only easy because Ray's parents had run a cafe, and although he had ducked out of helping them whenever possible it was inevitable that some skills rubbed off. He could finely chop an onion, for instance, in less than a minute and with his eyes shut to stop them watering. He preferred not to talk about those days. He gave Steve a fork, a paper napkin and a cup of tea from a flask.

'No wonder Dilly don't want to come home,' Steve said, 'not with grub like this on offer.'

'Oh it isn't the food,' said Ray, 'she can get food anywhere, she ain't fussy. Takeaways, ready meals, things in cans, stale bread, avocado face packs, it's all the same to your wife. What it is mate is, you two just need to clear the air. It's silly you carrying on like this, and we ain't really got room for her.'

'I s'pose,' Steve said, 'I always says the wrong thing though. Or sometimes I says nothing and that's wrong too and off she goes like a rocket. Best to leave her alone till she calms down I reckon.'

'Tell her straight. Tell her she got it wrong. Easy.'

'Oh yeah, same as you tell Margaret straight. About your finances and so on. That's easy is it?'

'Oh Margaret's a very different kettle of fish. For a start she never listens to a word I say.' Ray didn't want to admit to being scared of his wife. Steve was on to him though.

'You can't let yourself be scared of her,' he said, 'you're a man, right? Just tell her.'

'That's big talk. Tell you what, I will if you will.'

'OK, it's a deal.'

They shook hands on it and chewed on in comfortable silence. It was tasty food but in truth Ray would have much preferred a pub lunch with a beer or three. Still, he was driving and he had a plan for the money they'd saved on lunch. Plus he had Steve's petrol money jingling in his pocket.

'So,' he said, looking at his watch, 'how about we hit this on the head and treat ourselves to the football. If we go now we can get parked up, I know a little side street that always gets missed by the hordes.'

'Well truth to tell,' Steve said awkwardly, 'I was hoping for an hour up the library, that big job down the centre of town.' Only half joking Ray put his hand out and touched his friend's forehead.

'You must be coming down with something as my old Nan used to say.' Steve pulled away irritably.

'Don't be daft,' he said, 'I'm going down the library to look up 1887, right?'

'Nope, you've lost me. I mean I remember it because the Villa got relegated but...'

Steve explained at some length that he was talking about 1887 not 1987, and 1887 was the year of Queen Victoria's Golden Jubilee and also the golden age of steam railways.

'So,' he finished, 'I wants all my little people to be in the right uniforms for 1887, and I'm gonna make everything else proper for the whole layout, right, station buildings, little houses and so on, make some tiny little flag things, remember what we done a few years back, what was it, Ruby Jubilee? Street parties and all that. But I needs to see some photos from back then so's I get it right. I s'pose they did have photos back then?'

'I expect so,' Ray said, 'Now I do remember the last Jubilee. 1992. Margaret wouldn't shut the salon for the street party seeing as how it weren't official, neighbours sent us to Coventry, she wouldn't back down, I had to butter up the husbands down at the pub and they got their wives back on track.'

'We had a right do up our street,' Steve said, 'official or not. Cake. Jelly. Fizzy pop. Our Cheyenne was sick as a dog after.'

Ray dropped Steve at the Central Library and went to the football on his own. It wasn't his beloved Villa but it was better than looking through books about bunting.

******

Margaret and Dilys powered through Saturday with no time for awkward mentions of weight, grammar and spelling, or any surreptitious reference to wigs. But as they closed up there was one difficult conversation on the horizon.

'Erm, Dilys,' Margaret started, with uncharacteristic diffidence, 'the thing is, well, while you're in training, the thing is, about, you know, wages, I can't really, well the truth is, while I'm setting up my new business, but I'll make it up to you, I promise.'

Dilys hadn't thought about wages, except in a vague way. She wasn't used to having her own money. Before she was married her mum took most of her wages to cover the cost of her food and laundry. After she was married Steve gave her money to buy food and such, and when it was gone he always gave her more, but it never quite felt like it was hers.

'Pay me when you can,' she said with a shrug, 'I's still got some of me housekeeping left. Say what you will about my Steve, he's never kept I short. Oh dear.' And she started to well up. Margaret thrust a tissue at her.

'You earn that money,' she said, 'and don't you forget it. Don't let him treat you like a baby, Dilys. They're all the same, men, talking down to us like we're children.' Dilys blew her nose loudly.

'Oh they in't so bad,' she said, 'doing their best like the rest of us. But still, if you says so, I won't let him treat me like a baby. Mind you, I always think babies have it easy, no chores to do and lots of hugs. Food on demand. Whatever they want really.'

'I do say so, they're all the same, think they know everything. Well they don't, and we're empowered now and we aren't going to stand for it. Let's make a deal, no more standing for men and their nonsense. Right?'

'OK, OK I won't stand for it no more.' She picked up her bag, and was heading for the door when a thought struck her. 'I don't think I got enough money for a new dress, Margie, and I needs a new dress.' Shyly she took her jacket off and showed the gaping zipper.

'Breathe in,' Margaret said briskly, and she swiftly tugged the zip shut. Dilys gasped in shock, and Margaret smiled.

'Two days on your feet in the salon and look at the effect,' she said, 'like going to the gym only free.'

******

It was gone seven before Ray dropped Steve off at home. His secret parking place was all very well but you couldn't get out of the side street until the crowds had dispersed, and then there was the slight mix-up about where Steve was supposed to wait outside the library to be picked up which cost them half an hour. Neither of them were feeling quite up to the forthcoming discussions (Tanya for Steve and finances for Ray) but they'd promised each other and so it had to be done.

When Steve walked into the lounge-diner though Dilys was asleep on the couch in front of the TV, wrapped in her furry pink dressing gown. Her first full Saturday at the salon had exhausted her. On the screen a man with long hair and some sort of armour was riding a horse with a woman sitting in front of him, leaning against him feebly. Must be her Romance of the Month Club video he thought, they were always that sort of nonsense. He'd given her the subscription as a birthday present when she turned down his first idea of tickets for a Steam Fayre. He carefully prised the remote out of her hand and placed it on the coffee table, and threw her favourite fluffy yellow blankie over her. Then he crept out to the shed to unwrap his new purchases.

He was reprieved, until tomorrow at least.

Margaret was not asleep when Ray crept in but she was busy, upstairs in the living room surrounded by papers including their old account books and muttering to herself. Reluctantly Ray cleared his throat, and braced himself for the fray but without looking up she said 'not now Raymond, I'm doing my five year plan.' He went down to the kitchen and settled down with the last of the chicken pie.

He was reprieved, until tomorrow at least.

SUNDAY APRIL 21st

Sunday didn't start well for Dilys. She woke up early, still on the couch and feeling stiff and achy and cold. She had a quick bath with a cup of tea to warm herself up inside and out and felt a lot better. She was even ready to forgive Steve so she went down to the kitchen to organise their usual Sunday special fried breakfast. Since Margaret had told her not to be a baby she was going to tackle the Tanya issue head on. On a whim she ran out into the garden and picked a bunch of forget-me-nots and put them in a jam jar on the kitchen table. The smell of bacon wafted up the stairs and soon Steve appeared.

She put the plate down in front of him and waited for him to be grateful. He pushed the flowers to one side so he could reach the ketchup and through a mouthful of hash browns he said

'Gotta get an early start, Dil, I'm making a little row of Railway Cottages, look lovely at the back of the layout they will.'

'Steve,' she said, 'I needs to talk to you. About that… about… you know.' Steve looked puzzled, so she managed to force out the word 'Tanya'. He waved a forkful of egg. It was time to keep his promise to Ray and put the record straight.

'Silly misunderstanding,' he said, 'storm in a teacup. Don't you bother your pretty little head about it.' Dilys felt the overwhelming fury of an empowered woman, and one who was not a baby to boot.

'Oh silly am I,' she said, 'when me 'eart is broken, well we'll see about silly, oh yes, I'll show you silly and you can put that in your pipe and smoke it.' And she flounced out, leaving Steve to finish eating alone. He could tell she was upset, so he did the washing up before heading for the shed. He expected she'd probably appreciate him giving up twenty minutes of his precious modelling time.

Dilys barely noticed. She was scribbling furiously in her notebook.

******

Ray wasn't faring much better. Telling himself he was a man and definitely not afraid of his wife he waited till they were both eating breakfast. He placed himself at the opposite end of the table to Margaret, because he felt like it and not because it felt safer that way. Sunday was also a special breakfast day for Margaret so she had a grapefruit. He waited until she'd finished with the knife, then he laid a piece of paper on the table and pushed it towards her. It showed all his careful figure work regarding their finances, the costs associated with the bungalow, their potential income and so on.

'Have a look here, poppet,' he said, 'I've written it all out, the figures regarding the bungalow and our pensions. And I've kept it nice and simple for you so you can see how we're fixed.' Margaret finished her mouthful of grapefruit. She put down her spoon. She looked Ray in the eye for once.

'Simple am I,' she said, 'well I'll keep it simple for you too. I am NOT cashing up my pension. I AM having a new salon. And I will NEVER on my mother's grave live in that horrid little so-called bungalow.'

'But look,' he said desperately, 'look at the figures will you? It only works with your pension in the mix, it'll get us through till we can draw our State Pensions.'

'Get us through what? Staring at four walls all day instead of being out there in the world, doing something?' She remembered one of the speakers from the weekend and borrowed their catchphrase. 'Having a purpose, Raymond. Everyone needs a purpose.'

'Well my purpose is to enjoy my retirement. We've worked hard enough for long enough, Margaret, it's time to stop.'

'Oh piffle...'

- They were distracted by the doorbell, which Margaret went to answer expecting it to be Barbara. Then she remembered Barbara was busy.

It was Darin and his friend Ben. Margaret had summoned them via one of their mothers, who had been in for a dry cut (the cheapest thing Margaret offered, neither boy came from an affluent family). They appeared to be slouched against the doorframe but in reality they were propping themselves up. Their big sisters, both failed Saturday girls, had warned them about the fearsome Mrs. Boyles, but there was money in it and when you're twelve years old money is very tempting. To them Margaret was a dragon and they were heroes who were going to filch some of her hoard of gold.

The dragon opened the door and said

'Come in and for goodness sake do try to stand up straight.' She eyed them doubtfully.

'Was it really you two who sold Mr Boyles the computer and set it up?' There was some shuffling of feet and mumbling. Dragon slaying wasn't as easy as it looked on TV.

'What? I can't hear you, speak up. Did you do it?' Darin gathered up his courage and said

'It were me, Mrs Boyles.' Emboldened, Ben said

'It were his old one, what he got down the charity shop with his Christmas money, he's got a new one now what he...' Margaret wasn't interested.

'Very well. I shall give you a pound if you move it downstairs for me and another five pounds if you talk me through how to use it. When can you do it? Now?' More shuffling. They were already late for football, but the money, well, the money...

'Tomorrow?' she said, but they shook their heads. Monday evening was guitar lessons, paid for out of their meagre earnings doing odd jobs for neighbours. They were learning how to be rock gods as a sideline to heroing and playing football for England.

'Tuesday,' Ben said, 'us'll do it Tuesday. After school.'

'Be here at six,' Margaret said, 'on the dot mind. I shall dock you ten pence for every minute you're late' They looked puzzled so she added 'if you're ten minutes late you'll lose a pound, understand?' She opened the door and they scurried away.

Ray had washed up, in the vague hope Margaret would be pleased to see a tidy kitchen, and then gone upstairs to watch sport on TV. Not as good as the big screen in the pub but free because you didn't have to buy drinks. Margaret didn't notice. She gathered up her papers and settled herself at the kitchen table with pen and paper and resumed the struggle with her business plan.

******

Eventually the fit passed and Dilys reached the end of writing out how she felt about Steve calling her silly and the toasted cheese sandwich she'd needed for consolation. She'd never minded being silly Dilly before but this time was different, and she couldn't get her head round what had changed and what that Tanya had done to her marriage.

She'd started by writing that she'd needed the toastie to help her cope with the upset of Steve's behaviour and somehow that turned itself into a little story about a scarlet woman, who was Tanya except in a long frock with jewels and a fan, and how she broke the heart of the serving girl who was engaged to the handsome groom who looked after her horse but never mind, when the Tanya type dumped him he came back to her and she forgave him and he was happy to eat the humble soup she had bubbling on the hearth even though he'd had caviar and such when he was a rich Lady's plaything.

Wow, she thought, where did that all come from? And all that scribbling had made her feel peckish so she opened a tin of soup for her lunch so she could pretend to be the serving maid, but she didn't make anything for Steve. First he had to beg forgiveness on bended knee, like the man in her story. As she rinsed out the soup tin and the saucepan, she noticed the grubby sink, and it dawned on her that what with leaving home with a broken heart and starting her new career as an empowered woman and trainee hair salon manager she had fallen right behind with the housework, which she usually did in a leisurely fashion while Steve was at work. Why, she thought as she scrubbed the toilet, can't real life be more like a story?

******

In the salon kitchen Margaret was barely making progress with her finances, in fact she seemed to be going round in circles and every time she totted up the figures she got a different answer. This is harder than it looks, she thought, oh if only Raymond had any get up and go, he'd be doing all this. She went to find him so she could vent her feelings about his all round general uselessness, expecting him to be in the salon. Sunday was, after all, salon cleaning day. Every Sunday he would clean, and she would spend the day with her clothes. She firmly believed in buying good quality clothes and then taking the trouble to care for them. Hangers were padded, and most items had their shoulders covered with a protective layer of plastic to keep the dust off. Her shoes all had shoe trees, and were cleaned after every wear. Matching handbags were stuffed with tissue paper to keep the shape and also regularly treated with special leather enriching cream.

Once her clothes were in good order she would give herself a full facial treatment. After so many years of waxing everything she could reach she didn't have to worry about body hair, although she always checked. By the end of Sunday she always felt restored and ready for the week to come.

But there was no sign of Ray downstairs, and she could hear the TV upstairs so clearly he was skiving, again. She glanced round the salon, and realised that Dilys, who always seemed to have a cloth in her hand when she wasn't sweeping or scribbling, had kept pretty much on top of it. She threw some bleach down the toilet and went up to the sanctuary of her bedroom, where she soothed herself by putting her wardrobe to rights. She'd get back to the figures later.

******

Out in the shed Steve was realising just how much he'd spent at the model shop. There were new steam trains, tenders, carriages, all historically correct just needing a coat of paint. Some track too, even though there was no more room on the board that held his layout. Extra paints and brushes for decking out the little people he'd bought. A couple of signals. Even some model trees. What was I thinking, he said to himself, I'll be overdrawn for sure this month. Thank goodness for a steady job and regular wages.

And in the lounge-diner Dilys was realising that empowerment came at a cost. She was dusting her china figurines, a chore that she normally took slowly and with pleasure but now she was rushing because there was so much else to do, and one of the ears broke off her favourite doggie. I ain't sure about this working lark, she said to herself, week in week out, it's like a treadmill.

Margaret too was brooding, as she polished the clasp of her favourite patent leather handbag. Maybe I've bitten off more than I can chew, she said to herself, it really wasn't supposed to be this difficult.

In the living room Ray had found a channel with the London Marathon. Not his favourite sport but it would do. He wasn't saying anything to himself at all. As far as he was concerned that was what sport was for.

******

'You!'

It was Margaret who answered the door to Steve, not Ray as he'd hoped. Getting ready for work tomorrow he'd realised his wallet must still be in Ray's car so he'd asked Dilys to collect it on Monday for him and received a definite negative. So here he was.

'You!' That one word and that tone of voice sent Steve rocketing back to when he was fourteen years old and he was waiting outside the Saturday morning pictures for Dilys. No rosy nostalgia in this memory.

It was their first date. Or at least the first time they would do something just the two of them. Then this woman on the other side of the road shouted at him. He looked round at the crowd of waiting kids, hoping she meant someone else, but then she yelled 'Steven Richards!' and he knew it was him.

She was kind of chunky and her black hair was piled up in what his mum called a Beehive, held up there with back combing, hairspray and willpower. She crossed over and came closer and he realised it wasn't a woman at all, it was a girl from school, older than him and without her round National Health glasses. What was she called- Mandy? No, Maggie. It was only that Faggy Maggy, who was always hiding down the school field having a quick smoke with the other big girls. And her hair in pigtails, not sticking up like the funnel on a steam train making her look so different. Coo, he remembered the trouble when she dyed it black, came in on a Monday with it all black instead of mousey brown, and a black line on her face at the edge of her hair. She was sent home, but then they let her back, cos, like, what could they do? It was permanent dye, it'd last weeks and she had exams coming up.

Faggy Maggy. She was smoking one now, as she bore down on him. He looked round for help, but everyone suddenly was busy looking the other way. She took the bubble gum out of her mouth and spoke.

'Er in't coming, right? Er's up our house crying and 'er in't coming.'

'Why not,' Steve said, 'I got 'er toffees and everything.' He showed the bag of toffees in his hand and Faggy Maggy took them and shoved them in her pocket.

'It's on account of how you ignored 'er yesterday, at 'ome time. Walked right past, din't yer, never said a word.'

'I were with me mates.' Everyone knew the rules, when you were with your mates you didn't do soppy girl's stuff. Everyone knew that.

'So what, yah big Jesse. Anyway she in't coming and just you remember, I'll be watching yer, even when I leaves school I'll be watching, right?'

'Alright,' he said, and she walked away. With the toffees. But he went to the pictures anyway, and he spent the money he'd kept back for Dilys's ticket on an ice cream.

'Are you even listening to me?' Margaret said, and Steve shook his head and came back to 1996. Somehow Faggy Maggy had turned into Margaret Boyles, and once he married Dilys and she married Ray she seemed to take her eye off him, so that by the time they all went to Majorca together he'd pretty much forgotten that he'd ever been scared of her. Now it turned out she still had the power to frighten him.

He gathered up his courage. After all this was the woman Ray had faced up to and bested, so he couldn't let the side down. 'Come for me wallet,' he mumbled, 'left it in the car like.'

'Raymond,' she yelled, 'your weaselly little two timing friend is here,' and then, more quietly, 'you've done it this time. You aren't getting away with this one.'

Ray appeared, and Steve knew at once from the body language that Ray had not, in fact, bested her. It was clear she had very much bested him.

'Come for me wallet,' Steve said again, and Ray produced it from his pocket while Margaret stood by with folded arms and a grim expression. Then she shut the door in his face and Ray escaped back upstairs.

MONDAY APRIL 22nd

The salon was always closed on a Monday morning which gave Dilys time to have another look through her wardrobe, given the astonishing experience with the zip on her dress. One or two things were definitely closer to doing up than they had been, but nothing was quite there yet. There were dresses in there from years ago, from before Cheyenne was born, back when she used to try and have regular date nights with Steve.

Nostalgia threatened to overwhelm her as she remembered romantic walks on moonlit streets, wandering on the beach hand in hand, or sipping her cider while Steve played darts. Of course there was no Tanya then and they would often finish by picking up chips to eat on the way home.

Despite the distraction she arrived in good time for work, wearing a smart new skirt. Or rather an old skirt she hadn't worn for a long time. The elastic in the waist had long since given up the unequal struggle but she'd had the inspired idea of using a safety pin to attach it to her knickers.

Margaret pulled her into the shop.

'Thank goodness you're here' she said.

'I's early,' Dilys said, 'you said one o'clock and it's only just gone eleven.'

'I know,' Margaret said, 'but I have to go out and Raymond is never around when you want him and he's taken the car, I can't think why. I'll be back in good time for the pensioners, all you have to do is answer the phone and take bookings and remember what I said, Dilys - no chatting.' Ooh there's my taxi, must dash.' And she was gone leaping into the cab without waiting for it to come to a complete stop.

Ray had needed the car to get out to the doctor's surgery in Kingsford where he had an appointment. Margaret preferred them to use the small village practice, where she was convinced you got more personal treatment compared with the big surgeries in town. Certainly they had looked after her very nicely after that holiday in Majorca… but he didn't want to think about that right now, he had more pressing matters on his mind. He was lying on his side, knees drawn up, while Dr McDonald carefully inserted a gloved finger.

'Feels fine,' the doctor said after a few minutes, 'nice healthy prostate. You can get dressed now, Mr. Boyles.'

'So, doc,' Ray said as he hopped around on one leg, trying to get the other leg into his trousers, 'I wanted to ask you about my wife. Margaret. Mrs Boyles. I'm worried about her, and I know you saw her the other week.'

'If she's feeling poorly she should make an appointment,' the doctor said.

'Oh no, it's not that, but she's so, I don't know, full of beans. Like a Duracell bunny, she never stops. She never used to be like that.'

'Finding it a bit much are ye?'

'Well, yes, you know me, I like a quiet life, we were about to retire but now she's gone off like a rocket, full of plans and firing ideas left right and centre.'

'Book yourself in for a blood test, maybe you're a wee bit anaemic.'

******

Dilys had settled herself very comfortably at the desk with a coffee and her notebook and her favourite purple pen. There didn't seem to be any biscuits yet again so she was explaining how that made her feel, and why she didn't believe for one moment when Steve said there was nothing between him and Tanya which meant her heart was still broken and she really needed a biscuit, when she noticed the little book was nearly full.

She'd scribbled pages of nonsense, but it was what Margaret wanted so of course she would keep doing it, for Margaret's sake. Dilys had always been fond of Margaret despite, or perhaps because of, their differences and now she was a manager in waiting her feelings had moved up a notch. After all, Margaret didn't want much, she only wanted to keep her little salon, she'd put everything into it and now she was going to lose her heart's desire just so Ray could have his heart's desire and it was all a dreadful mess. Somehow Dilys had to help her friends through these terrible times, together they would heal the wounds, together they…

She nearly jumped out of her skin as the door flew open and a woman burst in, stopping in shock when she saw Dilys.

'Oh,' the woman said, 'you must be the new owner. Would you be so good as to get Mrs Boyles for me please? Tell her it's Barbara and could you hurry up, I haven't got long.'

'Er's gone out,' Dilys said, 'I'm Dilys. I'm helping Margaret out. Seeing as how we're old friends she's asked me to help while she's going through a time of troubles.'

'I've known Margaret for years and she's never mentioned a Dilys to me,' the woman said sharply. She was sharp all over Dilys thought, from her spiky haircut past her pointy red nails and down to her stiletto heels. Anyway she wasn't going to be outdone by any Barbara, not now she was empowered.

'Us was at school together,' she said loftily, 'was you wanting an appointment?' And she picked up her purple biro and the appointment book with a professional air, for all the world as if she knew what she was doing.

'I've already got one,' Barbara said, 'first Saturday of the month, every month, haircut and nails, and the other weeks I pop in on a Sunday evening so we can chat in private while she does my hair.'

'Sunday?' said Dilys, 'You wasn't around the other Sunday, I knows 'cos I come here as a place of refuge with me broken heart.'

Barbara glared at Dilys. She enjoyed her status as Margaret's best friend and she didn't like the look of the dumpy little scruff bag in the enormous denim skirt.

'I was in Torremolinos,' she said stiffly, 'we have a time share there. Very nice villa with a pool. I only wish I could get Margaret to join us there but apparently Raymond won't hear of it. That man has a lot to answer for. And yesterday I was out all day, so I missed my regular slot.'

'Me and Steve's very fond of Ray as it happens,' Dilys said with equal stiffness, 'and since neither of them's here right now and you aren't needing no appointments and as you can see I's very busy…' she waved the notebook vaguely. Barbara turned towards the door.

'Please be sure to tell Margaret I called by,' she said 'tell her I wanted to see if she'd been able to view the house. I'll call her later.'

******

Barbara as usual had jumped the gun. The taxi driver had taken the long way round and Margaret was only just ringing the doorbell of a large imposing house down a quiet lane in Kingsford. She would never normally think of living anywhere so grand but it was Barbara, whose neighbour had tipped her the wink that someone was looking for a house sitter, who put the idea in her head. The door swung open revealing an elderly women wearing a pink tweed suit and a cloud of perfume.

This is surreal, Margaret thought, I could swear that is Mrs Hetherington. Of course I haven't seen her since I worked in the village salon, must be what, 30 years ago? I wonder if she'll recognise me, I was a lot heavier back then and I had all that lovely long hair.

Mrs Hetherington clearly did not recognise Margaret because she greeted her in a friendly fashion which she would never have used for a mere hairdresser.

'Do come through,' she said, 'oh but would you mind awfully removing your shoes? This way please. Georgian niche!' Margaret was puzzled, but then realised that Mrs Hetherington was waving at a small inset shelf unit, with a crinoline lady in porcelain carefully displayed on it.

'Oh lovely,' she murmured. And she did rather like it, the spacious hall, the parquet flooring, the sweeping staircase. Much nicer than the bungalow!

'Now do come and meet my little Pooky.'

She led the way through to an elegant lounge, featuring wallpaper and curtains covered in enormous pink roses and where, curled up on a cushion, was a large Persian cat. It was wearing a diamante collar and a cross expression.

'I understand that you are a cat lover? I simply couldn't bear to leave him with anyone who didn't adore him. Pooky's opinion means far more to me than any references, although I shall require those too of course.' Margaret looked at Pooky and pulled her lips into a grimace that would have to pass for a smile. In truth she disliked cats, and the way they shed hair all over one's clothes, but that seemed only to mean that cats always took to her. She sat down primly and waited for Pooky to respond.

'You're looking for someone to house sit for six months I believe?' she said.

'That's correct, I've decided to take a world cruise, disembarking in Edinburgh where I shall visit my cousins, ever since poor dear Robert died my children have been begging me to leave the country, oh look I do believe he likes you.' Sure enough the wretched cat was winding itself around Margaret's ankles. She maintained her grimace.

'He's very sweet,' she said, 'I think we'll get along very well indeed.'

'He's mummy's precious boy, isn't he,' cooed Mrs Hetherington, 'shall we show Mrs. Boyles the rest of the house? Shall we?'

The cat did not deign to answer or to accompany them but Margaret liked it all, the spacious master bedroom with en-suite (the bath tap was a golden dolphin and the water gushed out of its mouth into a turquoise jacuzzi bath), the formal dining room with chandelier, even the ancient Hygena kitchen that was clearly Mrs. Hetherington's pride and joy.

'Is there a garden?' Margaret asked, because all she could see from the kitchen window was a large evergreen hedge.

'Yes,' Mrs Hetherington answered with a shudder, 'we have half an acre, but I had the gardener create that screen so we don't have to see the cows. It's a long story, and it needn't concern you, he will continue to maintain the grounds while I'm away so all you have to do is enjoy them and make sure Pooky stays inside. We don't allow him to mix with the local cats, such a common bunch. Now do let's go back to the lounge and discuss terms. What is it you do exactly? Are you a widow like myself?'

Ignoring the second question Margaret took the plunge. She was not going to lose this opportunity through being too common.

'I'm a business woman,' she said grandly, 'I specialise in… female well-being. I'm sure we both agree that a well-groomed woman is an empowered woman.'

'Oh indeed,' Mrs Hetherington said, patting her iron grey curls, which appeared to have the consistency of concrete, 'it's so distressing when you see these young women who hardly seem to bother these days, hair all messy, jeans, skimpy little tops.' Margaret nodded in agreement.

'…but, er, sometimes,' she went on, dropping her voice just like the frizzy haired woman, although unlike in the hotel only Pooky and Margaret could hear her, 'sometimes, well, I was saying to the girls at the Golf Club, only the other day, and of course as Ladies' Captain I take their welfare very seriously, but after a certain age, well…' Margaret knew exactly what was going on. If it wasn't weight, which it didn't appear to be for Mrs Hetherington was quite trim for her age, then it was facial hair, the curse of the post-menopausal woman.

'A little unwanted hair is easily disposed of,' she said smoothly, 'privacy cubicle, discretion assured, group discount rate.' She produced a business card. 'Do please all of you come and see me in my temporary premises, I shall be upgrading shortly but in the meantime let us not waste a moment.'

Mrs Hetherington took the card.

'Thank you so much,' she said, 'I'm truly grateful and OH STOP THAT AT ONCE!' Margaret nearly jumped out of her skin but Mrs. Hetherington had shot across the room to the picture window and was banging vigorously on the glass. Pooky fled under an occasional table and Margaret looked out of the window to see the taxi driver quietly smoking a cigarette in the front garden.

'Your driver,' Mrs Hetherington screamed, 'is shedding ash all over my dahlias.' She rushed out of the room and was to be seen berating the man, who coolly tossed his cigarette into the bushes, got into his car and drove away, leaving Margaret dumbfounded and stranded in Kingsford with its famously dreadful bus service. And she noticed it was starting to rain.

'Oh,' said Mrs. Hetherington as she returned, 'how very unfortunate. Still, the bus stop is at the end of our lane, I'm sure there will be one along shortly. Come along precious.' She was talking, of course, to the cat, who had retreated as far back under the table as possible and was now hissing at his besotted owner.

'Oh, yes,' said Margaret, 'I expect so.' It was clear that Mrs Hetherington was not going to offer her a lift, and as well as being too proud to ask, Margaret was determined not to lose the entire Ladies section of the golf club as customers. In fact...

'I suggest we strike while the iron is hot', she said, 'I tend to be booked up far in advance but I think with a little rearrangement I could see you and your group on Wednesday afternoon. Shall we say three p.m.?'

'That's very good of you,' said Mrs Hetherington, who was now on her hands and knees and half under the table herself, 'We shall see you then. Pooky do come to mummy there's a good boy.'

******

Having finished her coffee and her notebook, Dilys was reduced to wandering around the salon opening cupboards and peering into drawers. She couldn't remember where the new notebooks were kept but she thought perhaps she would turn one up, or failing that something to eat. She was brooding about that Barbara. Right hoity toity she was, her and her calling later. Still, it wasn't Barbara that Margaret turned to in her hour of need, oh no, it wasn't Ray neither. It was her, Dilys, and quite right too.

******

Steve was having a trying morning with a young apprentice who wanted to walk before he could run. In Steve's opinion even walking was probably beyond the lad, who seemed puzzled by the idea that a screwdriver had a handle end and a business end, which was for screwing screws rather than say, cleaning your nails or levering the lid off a tin of paint ('We has a paint tin lid lever for that task,' Steve had said more than once, to no avail).

He had enjoyed his quiet Sunday, although it was a shame to have to put all his model bits back in the shed. Unpacking his new purchases soon cheered him up though, and he had his notes from the library research to write up. He wasn't worried about Dilys, she always overreacted and now that she knew about Tanya things would, he was sure, soon be back to normal.

******

Ray had plenty to think about as he set off for home. While Doctor Macdonald, with many years of practice, had easily avoided breaking Margaret's patient confidentiality the same was not true of Simpkins. Ray had popped in on the off chance and found Simpkins and his receptionist Miss Dollymore with their heads bent over *Chicken Breeder's Monthly*.

'Thing is,' she was saying, 'our dad don't think much to bantams, but I likes 'em.'

When they noticed Ray they leapt apart guiltily.

'Ah,' said Simpkins, 'Mr Boyles, er, did we have an appointment?'

'No no,' Ray said, 'but I was over this way and I wanted to check one or two things with you.'

Simpkins took him through to the office and patiently went through all Ray's questions. Yes the salon was sold. Yes the new property was bought. No he couldn't change either deal. But there was one thing he'd been meaning to mention to Mrs. Boyles…

And driving home pondering on what he'd heard, Ray noticed a woman at the bus stop wearing exactly the same kind of old fashioned plastic rain bonnet that Margaret always kept in her bag to protect her wig from damp. Then he nearly jumped out of his skin, it *was* Margaret standing at the bus stop in Kingsford, looking forlorn and wet. Despite how things stood between them he would have to stop and pick her up, scuppering his plan to pop into the betting shop. Stibb the owner was an old friend and although Ray couldn't often afford a bet he always enjoyed the atmosphere of the bookies, as long as he could avoid the attentions of Miss Stibb, who lived with her brother over the shop.

He pulled up at the bus stop and Margaret climbed into the back seat. She wasn't exactly grateful but at least she didn't quiz him as to why he was in Kingsford.

'Step on it, Raymond,' she said as she buckled her seatbelt, 'I don't want to be late for the pensioners. We can't leave Dilys to cope alone.'

Ray drove on at his usual speed, on the basis that there was plenty of time, plus the salon was sold and soon the pensioners would have to take their custom elsewhere. Unfortunately they found themselves behind a tractor on one of the narrow Kingsford lanes. It was tugging a trailer loaded with silage and was going very, very slowly.

'Can't you get past him?' Margaret said, clearly frazzled.

'No,' said Ray, 'it's only a single width and there's a ditch either side.'

'Ditch?' said Margaret, 'for goodness sake, how long is it since you left Birmingham and you're still calling it a ditch? It's a rhyne, Raymond, a rhyne.'

'Well, Bab,' he said, turning his accent up to full, 'Oi don't care what yow call the bugger, you'll get just as wet if we go upsoid down in it.'

They crawled on in hostile silence. Ray decided this was not the best time to share Simpkins' news.

******

Steve was at his bench, puzzling over a jammed liquidiser, when the apprentice dropped a toaster which burst into pieces that flew everywhere. Steve did not jump out of his skin. He looked up and said with a sigh, 'fetch a broom'.

******

At the sound of the doorbell Dilys nearly jumped out of *her* skin *again*. Somehow she had fallen asleep on the treatment table in the cubicle, and now there was someone in the shop! She rushed out there, hoping it wasn't burglars or vandals. It wasn't either, it was worse. It was the pensioners.

Mrs Osbiston pushed past her, heading for the toilet, but the others were cackling about something.

'Cheese and onion flavour,' said Mrs Toogood loudly, and Dilys froze.

'Me and Steve,' the old lady carried on, 'used to have cheese and onion crisps sitting on the end of the pier watching the sun go down…'

She was only reading Dilys's diary! Out loud! To the other old ladies, who were chuckling happily. Outraged Dilys pushed her way to the front of the crowd.

'Ere,' she said, 'give that back, that's mine that is, private stuff.' But Dilys was small, and Mrs Toogood was rather tall. She held the little book up high where Dilys couldn't reach, while the others sniggered.

'He used to gaze deep into me eyes and once we wrote a message on the crisp packet and threw it in the sea. I wonders where that crisp packet is now? Perhaps it sailed to some far away land with palm trees and… oi, that hurt that did, I'm a customer, I know my rights.'

Desperation had given Dilys wings, or at least the energy to climb on a chair and grab her book back. Unfortunately it was a rotating chair and her weight caused it to swing violently and throw her off. She landed with a thump, but she still had a tight grip on her precious notebook. Unlike the safety pin, which chose that moment to part company with her skirt which fell round her ankles.

The ladies all howled angrily apart from Mrs Asker who couldn't take her eyes off the empty chair, which was still spinning gently. She grabbed it, climbed aboard and started to spin. 'Wheee,' she screamed, 'whee whee whee.'

Of course the others all wanted a go too and soon two old ladies were gyrating and screaming while the other two clamoured for their turn.

The chairs were creaking ominously. Then Mrs Trundle began to play with the spray tap on the hair washing sink. Mrs Osbiston appeared behind Dilys.

'She'll be sick,' she said, gesturing towards the gyrating Miss Stibb, 'she always is. Sick on the coach last week before we even got to Chocolate World. We was all sick on the way back of course.'

'Can you stop that please,' Dilys said, raising her voice over the screams and trying to ignore the draft round her legs, 'this ain't an amusement park and I'm sure Mrs Boyles will be back in a moment.'

Mercifully Miss Stibb stopped rotating.

'What about Mr. Raymond,' she said coyly, 'is he around?'

'Oh do be quiet, Enid,' said Mrs. Trundle, 'I've told you before, he ain't got no soft spot for you, it's his professional manner is all.'

'He always gives me the best cover up,' Miss Stibb said sulkily, 'and a cushion for my back.'

'What was that story all about,' said Mrs. Osbiston, 'I couldn't hear it all in the toilet but it sounded right good.' Dilys clutched her notebook to her chest.

'It's private,' she muttered, and took a step back, because the old ladies were advancing towards her. She tripped on the fallen skirt and landed with a bump on her bottom in the puddle left by Mrs Trundle's tap shenanigans.

The salon door opened and in walked Mrs Hetherington and her golfing buddies. She surveyed the half-naked woman on the floor and the five somewhat dishevelled pensioners.

'Am I in the correct place?' she said, 'we have an appointment with Mrs. Margaret Boyles, but I was given to understand it would be exclusive access.'

'I don't think so,' Dilys said, 'Monday is old lady day. It must be another day.'

'Oi,' said Mrs Trundle, 'who you calling old?'

'I distinctly recall Mrs Boyles saying that we should attend this afternoon. I was busy with my Pookums at the time but I…' She ground to a halt as Mrs. Toogood squared up to her. Dilys quickly stood up and stepped between them with a vague idea that she was responsible.

'What about that story?' said Mrs Osbiston.

'Yeah,' said Mrs Asker, 'it was right good.'

'Story?' said Mrs. Hetherington, 'in a beauty salon? Surely not.'

'It's got palm trees,' said Mrs. Osbiston.

'And food,' said Miss Stibb.

******

Steve was showing a visitor around the works. He didn't know why he was doing it but the boss was at home sick and so the job had fallen to him. They had inspected the shop floor, the Goods Inwards and the Goods Outwards and had arrived at the toilets. Strictly speaking the toilets weren't part of the tour but Steve was nothing if not thorough.

He had not been impressed a few years earlier when part of the toilets had been hived off to create a separate facility for the first ever female employee. It was nicknamed the Pink Palace - she'd even got a mirror in there! (And he'd been grudgingly forced to admit that she did have a way with a soldering iron). However that was history and he was now keen to show the visitor how modern and politically correct they were. He started with the Gents, saving the Ladies for a grand finale. As he opened the door a siren suddenly sounded, causing the visitor to jump out of his skin, and the sprinkler system sprang into action. Steve didn't jump. He wiped the water off his face. He said loudly 'Bob. What have we said to you about smoking in the toilets?'

******

When Ray and Margaret finally got past the tractor, and the sheep in the road, and the detour for roadworks, they found their pensioners sitting quietly, crammed in with Mrs. Hetherington and the entire Ladies section of the Golf Club, while Dilys, perched on the counter top and with a towel wrapped round her legs, read to them from her food diary. Margaret opened her mouth to speak but before she could start her apology several people said 'SHUSH!'

She shushed.

******

It was Margaret who let Steve in shortly before seven. He was clutching a carrier bag with some dry clothes for Dilys as requested. When Ray phoned him he was about to get out of his own wet clothes so he'd been a while, what with putting a wash on and hunting out some clean overalls for tomorrow. His plan was to give the clothes to Ray and then run before Margaret could attack him again. But once again it was Margaret who answered the door. He froze. She glared.

'Brought the clothes,' he said, 'sorry it took so long, had a bit of trouble parking, very tight space, missed that bollard by a hair's breadth, still, here you go.' And he pushed the bag at Margaret hoping to escape quickly.

He wasn't to know that Margaret was panicking. Steve was doing it now! Making those horrid hair-based remarks. He must know about the wig, of course he must, she'd never even thought of that before. Better mend some bridges, quick sharp.

'Come on in,' she said, relaxing the glare but not quite managing a smile, and she stood back to let him through. She looked tired he thought, and possibly, could it be, slightly squiffy? There was a scream of laughter from the kitchen.

'Jumped outta me skin,' came Dilys's voice.

'Me too,' said Ray, 'jumped outta my skin, and jumped right back in again.' And they both laughed uproariously.

Margaret grabbed Steve's sleeve and pulled him into the salon, slamming the door behind him. He followed her through to the kitchen. There was an empty wine bottle, several empty beer cans and three pizza boxes on the table. Dilys, who was wearing Margaret's second best negligée, grabbed the carrier bag and ran into the shower room. Margaret sat down and drained her glass of dry white wine.

'Steve, me old mate, me old mucker,' Ray said, 'sit yourself down. Have a beer. Have some pizza. Plenty left. We're all stuffed, well I expect Dilys would have a bit more, but I kept this back for you.' And he pulled half a pizza out of the oven. Steve took the beer but waved away the pizza.

'I don't like that foreign food,' he said, 'you know me. Strictly Brit. I am famished though, got any baked beans?'

'Oh go on mate, live a little. Go on, give it a go. Try a teeny little taste. Go on. For me. Go on,' and he pushed the pizza towards Steve. With a sigh, knowing it was the only way to shut up his inebriated friend, Steve gingerly took a small bite. Chewed. Ray and Margaret watched him expectantly. Steve swallowed. Took a swig of beer.

'So basically,' he said, 'it's fancy bread and cheese with a drop of tomato ketchup, right?'

Margaret started to laugh.

'Bread and cheese,' she said, 'bread and cheese, oh Steve, you're priceless.'

'So's your Dilly,' Ray said, popping another can, 'saved the day, no doubt about it.' And he told Steve the whole story, how Dilys kept everyone entertained reading her diary aloud while Margaret powered through three trims, five shampoo and sets and six top lips, and Ray made the complimentary coffees, handed her the tools she needed, persuaded the blue rinse and the perm that they looked so lovely they really could wait till next week, and still found time to nip out for cakes by way of compensation to the customers for the mix-up, which in fact was all Mrs.

Hetherington's and Miss Stibbs's fault but as we know the customer is always right.

By then Dilys was back in the room, wearing her tracksuit and blushing furiously. She sat down as far away from Steve as she could. But she couldn't stay mad at him for long. She'd always had a soft spot for the way his hair fell over his forehead, and the solemn face underneath the flop of hair. No wonder that Tanya wanted him! A few more sips of wine and she was ready to make eye contact across the table.

Unfortunately Steve didn't notice, he was deep into his third beer and was explaining to Ray in considerable detail why it was that the washing machine tended to trundle across the floor when it was spin drying a batch of towels. He also mentioned that as a domestic machine it wasn't designed to wash big loads of towels from a hair salon every single day, while at the same time Ray was explaining that cancelling the commercial laundry contract had saved shedloads of money and flogging the poor machine to death didn't matter because it was staying put, since the bungalow had a washing machine and fridge and cooker, left by the previous occupant who had gone to a place where such things are redundant.

'Thing is, young Steven,' he said, waving his beer can in a generous gesture that sent a fine spray bubbling up out of it, 'the thing is, you've got to act smart in this life, and you've got to be on the ball. A probate sale is worth waiting for, and when one comes along you need to get in there quick, see what I mean?'

'Ah well,' Steve said, 'we're council, no need to buy anything when you've got a council house.'

'And you see,' said Ray, carrying on regardless, 'the heirs want to get their money out ASAP so they don't haggle, and they leave you the white goods, plus carpets and curtains. They even left the wardrobe in the main bedroom. Nothing like a freebie, that's what I always say. Plus it was the only way we could've afforded the move.' He sat back, smiling. He had taken his eye off Margaret, the drunken fool. She put her empty wineglass down carefully and fixed her gaze on a distant point, probably somewhere in Siberia.

'The thing is, young Dilys,' she said, 'when your husband is a cheapskate, if you're not careful you'll find yourself living with green swirly carpets that look like pools of vomit, curtains that my granny would have thought were out of date, and a brown bathroom suite with a bidet but no shower, whereas, I, Dilys, am going to live in a house with parquet flooring, elegant fringed curtains with tasselled tiebacks, and a bathroom with gold taps where the water comes out of a fish's mouth. A fish Dilys, a gold fish.'

'Goldfish,' said Steve solemnly, 'can only remember things for two seconds. Or is it five?'

'Cakes!' said Ray, jumping up, 'we should finish the cakes, they're never as nice the next day.' He was suffering from the anaesthetic effect of alcohol and still hadn't noticed Margaret's fury and sarcasm. And he plonked a box on the table, with several doughnuts and Danish pastries nestling in the crumbs.

'Put the kettle on, Margie,' Dilys said, 'I needs a cuppa if I'm having cake.' Still simmering, Margaret slammed the kettle on and threw mugs onto the table with a clatter. No one noticed. She was exhausted and she gave up. Steve took another bite of pizza.

'Hmm, that old bathroom suite'll almost certainly be Imperial not metric,' he said. Ray nodded wisely, although that meant nothing to him. Margaret took a swig of wine and ate the cherry off a Danish - she was too tired and too angry to count the calories for once.

The kettle boiled. They made tea. They ate cakes. They finished the wine and beer. They had the last of the pizza. They opened more wine and beer.

'Look at the time,' Steve said, 'some of us has got work in the morning .' He stood up and swayed slightly.

'I'll drive,' Dilys said, also standing up and also swaying slightly. 'Oh but this's been fun, innit, like old times, the four of us together. Just like Majorca, d'you remember, whata lotta fun that were, us really let our hair down dinnum?' Margaret froze, suddenly sober.

'Not being funny or nothing,' Steve said, 'but I'm a better driver drunk than what you are sober Dilys.'

'Anyway,' said Margaret quickly, 'no time for reminiscing now eh? How about we call you a cab?'

TUESDAY APRIL 23rd St George's Day

Somewhere a phone was ringing. Something hard collided with Ray's head as he sat up to answer it. Somehow he had fallen asleep under the reception desk, behind the curtain, curled up on the cushions he kept there for when he needed to hide from Margaret. He crawled out gingerly but by the time he reached the phone, all of three feet above him, it had stopped and the answerphone was announcing in appallingly shrill tones that *We are closed* and *Please leave a message after the tone*. Ray sank down on the stool and put his head in his hands. A tinny voice declared that she was very sorry but she would have to cancel her nine thirty appointment as she was waiting in for the TV repair man.

Levering himself up, Ray tottered down to the kitchen where he drank a pint of water, disturbing the small animal that seemed to have made a nest on his tongue, and felt marginally better. He knew from long experience that food was the answer so he put two slices of bread in the toaster and sat down at the table and rested his eyes. As the toast popped Steve appeared. A vague memory surfaced, of there being no taxis available and Margaret hustling everyone off to bed.

'Toast, lovely,' Steve said, grabbing both slices, 'cor you looks rough, nearly as rough as that couch of yourn. Worst night's sleep I ever had. Bloomin' Dilly and her Don't you think you're sleeping in my bed. Just cos I told her the truth about her driving.'

'Can you quieten it down a bit,' Ray said, 'I'm feeling a bit fragile. Bad prawn on that seafood pizza I expect.' Steve laughed the ear splitting laugh of the moderate drinker.

'Nothing to do with prawns. Reckon you all had a head start on me,' he said, 'anyway, gotta go, I've only just got time to pop home and get a shave before work. Lovely to see you mate. Tell Dilly she can catch the bus home, she made I sleep on that ruddy couch so it's only fair. Tit for tat like.'

He was gone. There was no more bread and Ray was retrieving a yoghurt from the fridge when Margaret appeared wrapped in a frilly dressing gown and with her head in a towelling turban for all the world as if she'd washed her hair. She snatched the yoghurt out of his hand, looked round the kitchen and said

'Look at the state of this place, Raymond, and we open in half an hour.'

'No one sees the kitchen,' he said, 'and aren't you even a little bit hung over?'

'Certainly not,' she said, 'mind over matter, Raymond, mind over matter.' And she swept out. He sunk down at the table again and decided to rest his face on it for a minute. He had enough hangover for both of them. He was dozing off nicely when the smell and sizzle of something frying woke him up. Dilys was at the stove, with a box of eggs.

'Gotter mouth like the bottom of a parrot's cage,' she said, 'eggs is the answer. Eggs and tea.'

She was right, he knew she was right, but eggs frying made most appalling noise. He was just deciding to try standing up and then, if his legs would listen to him, leaving the room when Dilys said

'Is Marge up? Think she'd like an egg? Perk her up like?'

'She does not need perking up,' Ray said with a groan, 'she's driving me mad with her flaming perkiness these days. I wish I knew what's got into her. It's like she's got ants in her pants.'

'It'll be that HMRC,' Dilys shouted over the noise of the boiling kettle, 'them pills she's got in the bathroom cabinet. Her told I they made her feel full of beans.'

'But I do the books,' Ray said, 'why would she hide bills in the bathroom for pity's sake.'

Dilys wasn't really listening, she was busy arranging fried eggs on some of Margaret's apple flavoured low calorie rice cakes. She plonked some down in front of Ray, along with a mug of tea.

'Get yourself on the outside of that,' she said, 'you'll soon feel better.'

Margaret came in, dressed, made up, wig in place.

'Come on, Dilys,' she said, 'no time for breakfast, we've got a busy day.'

'Your nine thirty has cancelled,' Ray told her through a mouthful of egg, 'left a message earlier.'

'We shall have to start charging for late cancellations,' Margaret said. Ray forced himself to appear coherent. What Dilys had just told him was very disturbing.

'Never mind about that for now, pet,' he said, 'hiding your bills from me in the bathroom cabinet simply won't wash.'

'I have no idea what you're talking about,' Margaret said, 'the only thing in that cabinet are my pills. The HRT doctor gave me the other week.'

'What's he done that for,' Ray said, stunned, 'and why didn't you tell me?'

'I'd have told you if you'd shown the least bit of interest,' she snapped, 'all you did was drop me off at the surgery and sneak back round to see the solicitor again, and what did you say when you picked me up?

You said "Guess what, I've got us 500 quid off for that dodgy pipe in the kitchen."'

******

By mid-morning Ray had left for a restorative stroll on the sea front plus, possibly, the hair of the dog, and Dilys had asked Margaret if she could nip out and buy some tights, since the green sparkly ones were itchy and too small. She was back wearing yesterday's skirt and jumper. Underneath the jumper the skirt was now held up with Ray's elasticated belt and the neck of the jumper was adorned with a silk scarf of Margaret's, so she was looking and feeling smarter, but the tights were giving her gip. The salon was quiet for the next half hour, so Margaret said yes and told her to pick up bread and yoghurt while she was at it.

Of course she got distracted in the supermarket, pausing by a display of *Tastes of the Orient*. What, she wondered, was nasi goreng, and how would she get Steve to eat something he couldn't pronounce? She was nibbling on a free sample samosa when her eye was caught by a flash of peroxide blonde hair on the far side. It was only that Tanya, rummaging in a freezer without a care in the world! She emerged clutching a bag of something that looked like Yorkshire puddings and passed them to a young shifty looking bloke who was standing next to her. He popped the bag into his trolley, turned, and kissed Tanya on the lips. She giggled and threw her arms round him. Dilys couldn't believe it. Right there in the middle of the supermarket in full public view that little trollop was only two-timing poor old Steve! And with some chap with a big nose whose eyes were too close together. She was swept away by a tidal wave of conflicting emotions - outrage at Tanya's behaviour, pity for Steve, anger at Steve, pity for herself - it was more than one little heart could bear. Grabbing her basket she ran for the checkout, minus tights but with the bread, and the wrong sort of yoghurt.

At the salon Margaret was dealing with a phone call. Someone, young and female, had rung through and against a background of music and loud voices asked for 'our mum, 'cos our dad says she's there'. Margaret told the voice she didn't currently have any customers in the salon so perhaps she had the wrong number?

Just at that moment Dilys burst in, sobbing 'oh, oh, Marge, that Tanya…' and the voice said 'that's our mum, give her the phone can you?'

Margaret thrust the phone at Dilys, and whispered 'for you I believe, possibly your daughter.'

'Cheyenne!' Dilys squealed, 'baby, how are you?

'Mum can you call me back?' Dilys glanced across at Margaret, who was eavesdropping shamelessly.

'Er, no, sorry baby, I'm at work. And what's all that noise?'

'St George's day innit,' Cheyenne said, 'the Aussies are having a party but they've got no ideal mum, no ideal at all, listen, can you…'

'Party? At half past eleven in the morning?'

'It's midnight here mum, listen, I need you to…'

'Oh sorry baby, I'm a bit upset, there's this Tanya…'

'Tanya from school? Dolly's best friend? The one what's engaged to her brother Kieran, lovely lad, looks a bit like a chicken but you can't have everything can you? Must be from living with chickens all his life but his sister isn't like that, her's got a round face, looks like a teddy bear I always thinks.' Dilys thought about it while her daughter chuntered on - small eyes, beaky nose, he could've been a bit chickenish rather than shifty.

'Um, I dunno, she's bit older than you I reckon,' she said.

'That's right, coupla years above me, got together with Kieran Dollymore, erm, year eleven I'd say. Anyway mum…'

'But your dad…'

'You aren't believing that stupid gossip are you mum? Me and Craig's been having a right laugh about it, his mum told him all about it last time she phoned, but listen mum, this is costing me an arm and a leg, you're worse than dad you are, I want you to post me out my Union Jack knickers, OK?'

'What? Why?'

'Cos we're gonna throw a party and show them Aussies how it's done. And can you chuck in the bunting and stuff what you had for the jubilee. Gotta go now mum. Love ya!'

And she was gone leaving Dilys staring at the receiver. Margaret took it from her and replaced it on the cradle.

'I heard most of that,' she said grimly, 'I don't like the sound of any party where people get to see your knickers.'

And then their next two customers arrived so there was no more time to talk. Dilys quickly settled them with coffee, they were friends who always came together and liked to gossip while they were waiting.

******

When Johnson peeped through the window of Aphrodite's half an hour later he was astounded to see it was still functioning as a hair salon. Surely Boyles had said they would be closing immediately and moving out of the accommodation soon after? But there was a woman under the old-style dryer reading a magazine, and a smart little receptionist busily writing in a notebook - appointments maybe, or updating stock records. He liked to see staff nicely dressed and keeping busy. (He wasn't to know that under the desk she was bare legged and wearing her slippers, having finally given up on the itchy green tights and too small boots).

His plan for today had been to get a proper look at the premises from the outside and get a feel for the best way to market it. Now at least he could get inside, and maybe Boyles would show him round, so all the better. He'd bought it unseen, purely because his own bigger flashier new branch would soon be opening nearby, and having paid very little for it he now wanted to sell it on at maximum profit.

As he pushed open the door the receptionist looked up and gave him a dazzling smile - gold star, he thought, he was very particular about cheerful customer service in his salons as well as keeping busy and looking smart. (He wasn't to know that she had just written the final sentence of an entry - "He finished his ice cream and kissed I, and his lips tasted of choclit flake and I thought me heart would burst with happiness.")

'Good morning,' she said, 'how may I be of h'assistance?' He'd already glanced quickly at the floor, which was spotless. (A hair-free floor was his number one benchmark for a properly run salon even before keeping busy and customer service and dressing right, not to mention no gossiping between staff, no wasting product, very short lunch and tea breaks and, his personal favourite, move quickly to save time). Before he could answer, a woman emerged from the cubicle saying 'thanks so much Margaret, that feels so much better.'

And then behind her, the redoubtable Mrs Boyles who was about to reply when she saw him, and stopped in her tracks. Briefly she wondered if she had time to slip into her high heels instead of her smart but flat work shoes, that put her at a distinct disadvantage height wise, but he'd already spotted her and was advancing, holding out his hand, so she drew herself up as far as she could and made eye contact.

'Mr. Johnson,' she said icily, 'I don't believe you have an appointment. Dilys, would you check please and tell me if Mr. Johnson has an appointment?' Dilys, who was in the middle of giving the customer her change, glanced down at the appointment book.

'Mrs. Boyles,' Johnson said, 'how nice to see you again. I wanted to...'

'Nope,' Dilys said, 'we only got them little twins coming for their first ever cut, ah, bless their little hearts...'

'Thank you, Dilys,' Margaret said, before Dilys could get onto the lock of Cheyenne's hair that she kept from her first cut and put in a locket, 'that will be all,' and then, to Johnson 'Dilys is training to be a manageress. We're making progress, but still a way to go.'

Johnson gave her a wry smile.

'Tell me about it, I always say training staff is like herding cats,' he said, 'anyway, is your husband available by any chance?'

'My husband is a very busy man' Margaret lied, 'he's seeing someone today and I'm afraid I have no idea when he'll be back. And as you can see, I am also busy so if that's all…'

She stepped forwards at the same time as the door opened on the young mum with the twins in a double pushchair. Somehow Johnson found himself being edged out as the twins were carried in, and the door being firmly shut on him. The woman was formidable, no doubt about that, but also no doubt that she could run a decent salon.

******

When Ray answered the doorbell at one minute to six he interrupted Ben and Darin who were wondering if they'd get an extra ten pence because they were one minute early. He vividly remembered what it was like to be that age, plus he had a feeling they were in for a difficult evening, so he slipped them a fiver and told them to keep it quiet.

Once Margaret had issued her orders he watched silently while the boys moved the computer down to the Reception desk and set it up there. When Margaret started fine tuning its position, making sure that the clients could see the receptionist and the receptionist could see the screen, he went back upstairs to watch TV with Dilys, who seemed to have left home again. He had found the thing useful for doing the books, but he didn't really care whereabouts he did that job, which took him precisely one hour a week. The accountant did the rest. However he'd also enjoyed playing various games on it, all the while giving the impression, without actually lying, that he was busy with the accounts, but really that was all history now.

Margaret sat down to listen. Darin did most of the talking. He was the tech enthusiast, and he wanted to tell Margaret all about RAM and ROM and floppy things but she soon put a stop to that.

'I only want you to show me what to do to make it work,' she said, 'start from the beginning.' Darin started from the beginning. Margaret took it all in, and asked him a load of questions. Half way through when it started to get complicated she grabbed a beauty diary and started making notes.

Along the way she learned all the things it couldn't do because it was 'so old' - all of five years. There were many amazing things, apparently, that a newer model would bring into her life. These seemed to be mostly to do with games, but when Margaret said she never played games the boys muttered something about the World Wide Web, and spreadsheets. Margaret didn't care. She now knew how to save her business plan onto a floppy disc which was a big step forward from starting from scratch every time, and she could see her way to a simple appointment system. That would do for now.

She paid them and said 'what do you say boys?' She was a big believer in teaching the young good manners. 'Thank you, Mrs Boyles,' they both muttered, although Darin was thinking rebelliously it was money they'd earned, not like a present or anything. She didn't notice, she was looking at Ben's hair, because his hoodie had slipped off.

'Who cut that?' she said crossly, 'it looks terrible.' They exchanged glances, neither of them wanted to mention their sisters, spectacularly and simultaneously sacked because neither of them would admit to causing the cigarette smoke in the kitchen, which doubled as the staff rest room. Their sisters were in disgrace at home as a result, grounded and expected to cut everyone's hair as well as doing chores.

'Oh sit down,' Margaret said, 'not there, that's for waiting, sit here, facing the mirror. If you ask me bad manners and bad haircuts are ruining this country.'

'Can you make us look like Ant n Dec?' Darin said eagerly, 'I could be the fringe one and he could be the brushed back one.'

'That's perfectly ridiculous,' Margaret said as she wrapped him in a cover up.

'Oh please, Mrs. Boyles,' Ben said, putting on his best sad face, 'we never get to have a proper haircut.' Margaret remembered all too vividly what it was like to be young and broke, and her mother cutting her hair in the kitchen with the old blunt scissors that she also used for cutting the rind off bacon. She got the clippers out and made them both look smart, and vaguely Ant n Dec-ish.

At the door Ben, emboldened by his new look and the knowledge that freedom was only two steps away, piped up 'please tell your friends about us won't you? We're really good at computer stuff me and Dazza.'

'Alright,' Margaret said, thinking of Barbara, whose dinosaur of a husband didn't believe in having new things. Even their TV was black and white, but she knew Barbara would love to get one over on him by having her own computer.

Little did she know that in the space of a couple of hours she had set Ben and Darin on their future path, running their own IT company. Ben would do the schmoozing and use his charm to bring in the customers,

Darin would be the techie whizz with zero social skills who sorted out their computers. They would employ an accountant to handle the money though.

WEDNESDAY APRIL 24th

The one and only Wednesday morning client had left and Dilys was sweeping up while Margaret surveyed the new computerised booking system that she had created after Ben and Darin left. It looked just as empty as the paper system they were currently still using until Dilys got the hang of the computer. It was a depressing sight and Margaret was not in the best of moods. Ray had gone AWOL again and she had no one to take it out on.

'You know what,' Dilys said, pausing for breath and leaning on the broom, 'susposing there were a power cut. That there computer won't work, will it, if we gets a power cut, then where'll us be?'

'We never get power cuts,' Margaret said grumpily.

'1987!' Dilys said triumphantly, 'four days in January with no power after that big storm, I remembers because it was our Cheyenne's birthday and we had to cancel the party. When the power come back she were in a sulk about it and she went off to the park with her mates instead.'

'Yes,' said Margaret, 'and I had to close anyway because there was no hot water and no power for the dryers. Really, Dilys you should think before you speak.'

It was a nasty thing to say and Dilys had to gulp back the tears before she could reply. She was getting better at fighting back though, and she dredged up a retort.

'Maybe next time you gets your pensioners and golfers all muddled up instead of helping out with me diary I'll tell 'em No, Mrs Boyles says I gotter think before I speaks. Tell you what, maybe I'm not good enough for you, maybe I'll just get outta your hair right now.' She reached for her coat, and Margaret realised she'd gone too far and sent Dilys back to making loaded remarks about hair. She took a deep breath.

'I'm sorry,' she said with an effort, 'you're quite right, you saved the day. But of course they come here for our extensive range of grooming treatments, not for entertainment.' Dilys's fight back soon crumpled.

'No you're right,' she said sadly, 'I'm not good for much am I. Steve always used to tell me to never mind, cos I was the pretty one, but you don't stay pretty forever do you? At least you got a business.'

There was an awkward silence. Margaret knew she had never been the pretty one and it still rankled. Dilys picked up a magazine and put it back on the pile. She was already anxious to make the peace.

'We need some more of they,' she said, 'I've read 'em all. I read the one with the prince in disguise three times.'

'They're for the customers, not that they bother with them much,' Margaret said, and also keen to restore harmony she added 'They'd probably prefer your diary.'

'That Mrs Osbiston gave us a tip, five pound,' Dilys said, and added quickly, 'I put in in the tip box. You were washing your hands at the time.'

'Good grief,' said Margaret, 'the pensioners never give tips. Never. Five pounds!'

Dilys began to laugh.

'Tell you what, I could do a new bit every week,' she said, 'keep 'em coming in for more. I could stop when I gets to a good bit and then they'd have to come back next week for it, like in the mag, look, there's always a serial see, and it always stops just before the good bit and then you have to look through the pile for next week's one…'

'Alright,' Margaret said, 'give it a go.' Dilys looked astonished.

'Aw no, I was only joking,' she said, 'but anyway I needs a new notebook for the food diary. Finished this one see? Full of nonsense it is too.'

Margaret pulled one out of the desk drawer.

'There you are,' she said, 'do another instalment before next Monday and let's see how they like it. Right, now I'm running out for an hour or so, we've no more clients till four. I'm seeing a few agents about the new salon.'

******

As Margaret left full of hope of finding a new salon in a better location but at a low rent, Ray was just giving up on his own hopeless quest. It had occurred to him that a new bathroom suite might tempt Margaret into moving so he'd visited a couple of plumbing supply stores. Bathrooms, it appeared, were unbelievably expensive, even the cheap ones. Only one place had even heard of goldfish taps, and they had to look it up in an old catalogue - very 1980s apparently, apart from the prices of course. He decided to console himself by having lunch with Steve. It was drizzling so they sat in Ray's car.

'Time was,' Steve said mournfully, 'you could've come in for a warm round the stove but now it's all Health and Safety and new rules all over the place and they ripped the stove out because of the fumes or some such plus no visitors allowed without getting special pass.'

'Yeah,' said Ray, 'so what about my bathroom problem. Can you paint a bath?'

'Might be possible,' said Steve, 'you can paint almost anything with a specialist paint, take my models for instance, course there's the rubbing down, and you needs several coats…'

'Sounds like a lot of work' said Ray, 'maybe I'll just, erm, I dunno, jazz it up a bit. Cushions. She likes cushions.'

'Not in a bathroom mate, here, tell you what, I could make her a soap dish, got a spare tender and an old loco what doesn't run any more, she could put her soap in the tender, right, where the coal ought to go.'

Silence while they both imagined Margaret retrieving soap from a toy train.

'Prob'ly not,' Steve said, 'anyway I uses if for odds and ends in the shed. Always coming across screws and washers and suchlike.'

'She'll just have to lump it then,' Ray said, 'it's got a nice little cupboard for her pills, she'll like that. Did I tell you she's on that HRT?'

'Bloke at work told me it's like Viagra for girls.'

Silence while they both tried not to imagine that.

'There's your answer though,' Steve said, 'it's pepped her up like, new lease of life. Anyway, better go back in, something funny at work today, can't put my finger on it, but things ain't right.'

'You're the foreman, wouldn't they tell you if there was something going on?'

'Well yeah, prob'ly. Seeing the boss at three actually, prob'ly I'll find out then.'

'Not probably, mate, definitely. You're too soft you are. Make it clear you won't stand for any nonsense, right?'

'Yeah, you're right. No nonsense. But I aren't doing no deal with you this time, all I got last time was Dilys doing her nut again. Mind you, maybe you're too soft on Margaret. Tell her she should be glad to have a roof over her head and stop being a princess. See how she likes that.'

Steve set off across the car park and Ray headed back to the beach.

******

Margaret decided to be choosy about which Estate Agents she patronised. The one who sold them the bungalow, for instance, was distinctly down market with a small office in a scruffy side street. She could not imagine that he would handle the kind of high class establishment she envisaged for her new salon so she wouldn't bother with that one. She targeted the bigger agents on the High Street and gave them her very detailed wish list. They took her contact information but were not very encouraging. All the prime spots, it seemed, were taken, mostly by chains selling fast foods or cheap clothes.

******

It was easy to give Steve advice Ray realised, but harder to work out what to do about the bungalow. And so, after a long think and a stare at the sea, he admitted defeat. There was no way he could be any tougher on Margaret, and he knew from years of experience that she was tougher than him anyway. Before he could change his mind he called into the agent who had sold it to him and said he'd be putting it back on the market as his plans had changed.

'Ah,' said the agent, 'I suppose you're another one who's retiring to Spain. It's not all it's cracked up to be you know.'

'I know,' said Ray, 'had a holiday there once, far too hot for me. No we're staying here, but not in the bungalow.'

'I'm afraid you won't get what you paid for it.'

'What?'

'Yes I'm sorry, but the market's dropped off something terrible, what with all the new builds coming up, people are spoilt for choice, and they always prefer a shiny new place to a tired old one. I suggest we reduce by ten percent and hope for the best. I'll get right onto it.'

'What!'

Ray stomped back to the salon where he found Dilys deep into writing in her new notebook. She looked up when the shop bell rang, but went straight back to it when she saw it was him.

'Alright, Dil?' he said, hoping for some soothing words before he faced his wife.

'Mmm,' she said, 'is soul mate all one word, Ray?'

'Search me,' he said, and headed upstairs.

******

Meanwhile Margaret was having coffee with Barbara.

'Those estate agents are all useless,' she was saying, 'not one single suitable premises between them. What's the point of calling yourself a property agent if you haven't got any properties? I'd be a fine sort of hairdresser if I didn't cut hair.'

'Mmm,' said Barbara. She had other things on her mind. Or rather one thing. Dilys.

'You never mentioned this Dilys to me,' she said, 'Didn't seem like your type at all.'

'Oh,' said Margaret dismissively, 'it all goes back to school. Long before you moved here. We lived on the same street and I used to walk her to school. She's a couple of years younger than me you see.'

'Hard to believe that,' said Barbara loyally, 'she's let herself go I suppose.'

'Anyway, I hadn't seen her for years until a couple of weeks ago. I know she's flaky but, well, you know, we go back a long way. I'm training her up to manage the new salon for me. I'll be expanding you see, I'll need staff.'

'Alright,' said Barbara, reassured that Dilys was only staff, 'tell me more about this jacuzzi bath. It sounds wonderful. Did you see it in action?'

******

By the time Dilys reached home that evening she had completed a long fantasy in which Steve featured as a handsome millionaire who fell for her over a doughnut when his car broke down outside the bakery where she worked. It was based, she felt, on the truth, apart from the millionaire bit. And the bakery bit. And the bit where he gazed deep into her eyes and she wiped the sugar off his chin and he swept her to off to a beach with palm trees. In any case writing it had cheered her up no end and she was ready to be friends again.

She found the real Steve sitting on the sofa, holding a letter.

'Have a look at this here,' he said, 'it's a rum do and no mistake.'

'Dear Mr Richards,' she read
'Further to your meeting with HR this afternoon I am enclosing details of our redundancy plan. The offer of alternative employment will remain available for four weeks from the date of this letter.'

'I don't get it,' she said, 'what's wrong with your old job?' Steve sighed.

'Closing us down ain't they,' he said, 'building houses on it, moving the works out into Somerset somewhere. Middle of nowhere. I in't driving out there every day. Reckon I'll take the money and run.'

'Oh,' she said, 'I am sorry, Steve, after all them years. Heartbreaking for you. How about I make us a nice bit of sausage and mash? Fried onion? Few peas?'

'I've lost me job, Dil,' he said, 'you can't fix everything with food.'

'People gotta eat,' she said indignantly, 'cept Margie of course, her barely eats anything, 'ere, she were in a right snit when she come back from looking for her new salon, nothing out there she said. And Ray come home, face like thunder,….'

'He's got a few bathroom problems that's all.'

Dilys pulled out the frying pan and the sausages. It was teatime after all, and they still had to eat whatever Steve said. She was struck by a thought.

'Poor Bozza,' she said, 'that's the end of her food van I 'spect. They won't want a food van on a housing estate will they? Lovely burger she did too.'

'Oh she'll be OK,' Steve said, 'her old man's got that ice cream van, remember, I fixed the chime for him one time. Right little gold mine that is.'

Dilys was leafing through the other papers attached to the letter while she waited for the pan to heat up. A small sum of money was mentioned as Steve's redundancy payoff.

'Ooh,' she said, her head suddenly full of palm trees 'let's use it to go to Australia, visit our Cheyenne, won't cost us much when we're out there, we only needs the air fare.' As far as Steve was concerned Australia might as well be on the moon. He hadn't been on a plane since Majorca and that suited him just fine.

'No, Dilys, no,' he said, 'we ain't frittering it, money's tight right now because, well, never mind why, and besides I needs a bigger shed, Cheyenne knows where we are if she wants us.'

The palm trees crumbled to dust. Dilys burst into tears.

'Give it a rest for Pete's sake,' Steve said crossly, 'you ain't lost your job.'

'No,' she sobbed, 'but oh my heart is broken...'

'That's enough!' he shouted, 'I'm sick of all this nonsense, do you hear me? We're gonna make some changes round here, and I'm gonna have a bit of peace and quiet if it's the last thing I do.'

Dilys stopped in mid sob. Nothing like this had ever happened before. Steve stomped off to his shed. He was going to sleep in Cheyenne's room whether Dilys wanted him to or not.

******

Just before she went to bed Margaret tidied the kitchen, and under the local paper she found some post. Mostly circulars but one was for her, from the bank.

Dear Mrs. Boyles, she read,
Further to your loan application, I regret to inform you that this has been rejected.
Yours etc.

She wasn't to know that the bank manager had taken the simple route of doubling his cleaner's wages and thus buying her silence, but in any case blackmail wasn't in her nature and she had only been bluffing. The truth was she never really listened to the cleaner's scandalous gossip. It was probably no worse than all the other stories customers told while she was working. So no bank loan. She would have to find another way. She would find another way. She was not going to be beaten.

THURSDAY APRIL 25th

Neither Ray nor Margaret were their usual ebullient selves over breakfast. Margaret started the hostilities. She needed to work out some of the anger she felt about the bank loan and Ray was always her preferred whipping boy.

'Those so-called property agents,' she started, 'haven't got a brain cell between them. One of them even suggested I could rent an industrial unit, not a nice one mind, one of those near the station. It's an old Nissan hut! Left over from the War! Can you imagine me cutting hair in one of those old wrecks? I blame you for this Raymond. If you hadn't sold my salon from under me…'

Ray was still smarting over the news about the bungalow. And still wondering how to tell Margaret. He now had two pieces of difficult news for her.

'Our salon,' he said sulkily, 'our salon, and you signed. I can't help it if you didn't bother to read the thing.'

'My mother always told me you were a waste of space,' she said, 'all mouth and trousers, that's what she said. She was coarse but she was right. But I will have another salon, Raymond, I will.'

Ray had had enough. He had courted Margaret's mother almost as much as he had wooed Margaret, and he considered he'd been an exemplary son-in-law. Anger gave him the courage to finally tell her the solicitor's news, which he chose as the more likely to cause maximum grief, since she didn't care about the bungalow anyway.

'You won't be having a new salon. Not in this town,' he said, and he felt an unpleasant surge of triumph.

'What?'

'It's in the contract. We can't open up within five miles of any of Johnson's branches for the next five years. And he's got branches everywhere.'

'What!'

'Yes it's an unusually onerous clause, but I thought we were retiring, and he paid an extra ten grand. I'd forgotten all about it till…'

And then, seeing that Margaret was about to explode, Ray abandoned his anger and his explanations and made good his escape.

******

Dilys refused to speak to Steve, which was easy as he was still in bed when she left the house to catch the early bus. And by the time she arrived at the salon, with her tear stained face and back in her oldest tracksuit, Margaret had staged a recovery of sorts. She was determined to find a way, and the obvious answer was to arrange a meeting with Johnson and charm him into giving her what she wanted. She wasn't very interested in the Steve story, in fact she suggested that Dilys was better off without him.

'But I'm a woman what needs a man,' Dilys wailed, 'I needs choccies and flowers and suchlike.'

'And Steve gave you those did he?'

'He might change,' Dilys said sulkily, 'you never know.' Honestly, Margaret thought, will she ever get what it means to be empowered.

'He won't change, all he cares about is his stupid shed and his even stupider toy trains,' she said, 'this is what you're going to do. Go home and start packing. Tomorrow I sign the contract with Mrs Hetherington, six months' rent free. It's a big house, five bedrooms, plenty of room, you move in with me and we'll work out what to do next.' In her mind's eye she had already put a lock on the bedroom door, so that she could deal with her wigs in privacy. In most other ways sharing the house, and especially the cat duties, with Dilys, could work out very nicely.

'What?'

'And what's more, we'll type up one of those stories of yours on the computer and send it off to that magazine. Come on, you read it out and I'll type and put it into proper English. We've got twenty minutes before the first client arrives.'

'What!'

An hour later, having posted off her story first class, Dilys let herself into her house. She hadn't actually agreed to move into the Kingsford house but Margaret told her to go home anyway, as she wasn't in a fit state to work. She was astonished to find Steve sitting on the settee in the lounge-diner. He looked up at her, white faced. There were tears in his eyes.

'Oh, Dil,' he croaked, 'what am I gonna do?' Dilys gasped, horror washed over her.

'Not Cheyenne,' she whispered, 'please, no.' Steve swallowed and took a deep breath.

'It's me shed,' he muttered, 'me shed. Twenty five year I've had that shed. And then the postman brings I this. Couldn't eat me toast. Couldn't face work.' Dilys took the letter from his shaking hand. It was from the Council's Housing Department.

'Dear Mr and Mrs Richards' she read *'Subsequent to the eighteenth birthday of your dependent child in October of this year the*

council will be obliged to serve you with notice to quit your two bedroom property.
    The council is pleased to be able to offer you rehousing in a suitable one bedroom property, as below:
    Flat 421
    4th floor
    Brunel House
    This property is currently being fully refurbished including new double glazing and will be available to you with vacant possession the Monday following the birthday of the aforementioned child.
    Please find attached a schedule showing your new rent and date of transfer. Please sign and return the top copy, retaining the bottom copy for your records.
    Yours etc'

    'Oh,' she said, 'Brunel House. It's nice up there, Mike and Mary lives up there, ground floor on account of her arthritis, still it's got a lift. Nice views from the fourth floor I bet.'
    'Me shed,' Steve moaned.
    'Seems strange,' Dilys said with a sigh, 'to think of our Cheyenne's turning eighteen, and her so far from home, living out her dream…'
    'Me shed,' Steve said again, 'nowhere to put the layout. Them flats is like shoe boxes. Oh Dil, what am I gonna do?'
    Something in Dilys snapped and rage swept her away.
    'Oh put the damn thing in the lounge,' she said, 'I don't care.'
    'What?'
    'I'm moving in with Marge. 'Er's got that house in Kingsford. Five beds and a jacuzzi bath.'
    'What!'
    Leaving Steve with his mouth hanging open she stomped upstairs to pack. As she threw clothes randomly onto the bed she began to imagine herself living in a posh house in Kingsford. Every day after work, she promised herself, she would have a bubble bath in that fancy bath, with the tranny on her favourite station and a large piece of cake balanced on the side right next to her, and a magazine of course. Her and Margie would eat their tea in the dining room, she'd never had a dining room but she was sure it had a long shiny table and a blazing fire in winter and maybe even a chandelier. In the summer of course they would eat out on the terrace. Soon she would be a proper Manageress in Margaret's swanky new salon and Steve, well Steve, he'd be up Brunel House with his trains and he'd have to find a new chip shop and serve him right.

******

Margaret had a busy afternoon with neither Dilys nor Raymond to help her, which left no time to think through the dreadful news about the salon. She only knew she would find a way, somehow, even if it meant moving to another country. Wales for instance, was just across the water and no doubt they needed hairdressers same as everyone else. There would be time to work it all out once she was settled in her new accommodation.

She had dealt with her last customer and was getting ready to close up when Mrs. Hetherington burst through the door.

'Oh, Mrs. Boyles!' she cried, 'the most terrible thing has happened!' She seemed unable to continue, so Margaret took control of the situation.

'Now do calm yourself,' she said smoothly, 'a little regrowth is only to be expected. I could deal with it now…' but Mrs. Hetherington was shaking her head violently, and she clutched Margaret's arm.

'No,' she gasped, 'it's not that. It's… Pooky! Poor dear Pooky.' And she choked down a sob.

'Oh,' said Margaret, thinking of a blissfully cat free house but managing to plaster on a serious expression, 'I am so so sorry. I hope he didn't suffer?'

'Terribly,' said Mrs. Hetherington, 'but so so bravely. As the vet said to me, Mrs Hetherington, he said, that is a most remarkable cat. A lesser animal would surely have succumbed. Of course he will need the best of care as he recovers.'

'Oh,' said Margaret, her head now full of unpleasant images of cat nursing.

'I knew you'd want to know straight away, seeing how strongly you feel for the poor thing. And I promise you, as soon as he's on the road to recovery we shall invite you over to visit him. You'd like that I'm sure.'

'Yes,' said Margaret, 'of course, but, er, won't you be on your cruise?' Mrs Hetherington stared at her, aghast.

'You surely can't think I would leave him at a time like this? No, I shall have to cancel it. I shall claim on the insurance so I won't be out of pocket.'

******

Ray was so miserable at lunchtime that he couldn't be bothered to eat his sandwich, so he threw it at a passing seagull who caught it with an elegant swoop. The tide was out and beyond the strip of sand were acres of dark sinking mud. Legend had it there was an entire coach and horses lost in the mud one time. Or was it a tractor and trailer, he wasn't sure. Whatever it was, he felt like his life had gone the same way, sucked down into the mud, drowning.

He considered his options. There would be some money left over from the sale of the bungalow, but not much once the expenses were paid. And Margaret would want half of course. He wasn't the sort of bloke who thought about relationships much. It was more like Margaret was a fact of life, always there whether he liked it or not. But now he wondered if the marriage hadn't gone down in the mud along with everything else.

People were getting divorced all over the shop weren't they. Not just famous ones like the Royals either. He knew that from the salon, when the divorce was going through you wouldn't see a woman for a while, then when it was settled she'd be back, her hair lank and uncared for, and demanding a new look for her new life. She usually left with highlights and a manicure, looking ten years younger. And the man would be seen at the pub buying a pie because he couldn't cook. More often than not they found a new person to be with, both the men and the women. In other words, people went down then they came back up again.

But no, he didn't want a new person and all the palaver that would involve. He wanted a quiet life, no worries, and enough money to get by. He'd simply assumed that Margaret would want that too, but she didn't. He thought of Brum, where his cousin was now running the family cafe. He was always in need of someone to do the washing up. I'd rather, thought Ray, sleep on the beach and scavenge in dumpsters.

******

Steve was so down he was beginning to understand what Dilys meant by a broken heart. When he went into the kitchen to make lunch (b on t, of course) he couldn't bear the sight of his shed out there, silently waiting for him, with its deep patina from years of creosoting and state of the art heavy duty padlock, plus of course security hinges on the door and external bars on the window. Now all that effort was for nothing and the faithful old shed would be left for the new tenants, who would stick a lawnmower and a paddling pool in there without a thought for its past glories. He'd be stuck in a tower block on the edge of town, and no, he wouldn't set his track up in the lounge because a) it would be too small and poky, they always were, and b) sooner or later Dilys would be back, she always was. He too didn't think about relationships, Dilys was a fact of his life and it never occurred to him that she wouldn't come home. He never read the news, Royal or otherwise, and he hadn't got a salon or a pub to teach him about life, the universe and divorce.

He closed the blind so he didn't have to see the shed but that was no good, the image was still there, burned into his brain. He was so fed up he went into work for the afternoon, just to get away. But work was another place that held no satisfaction for him anymore. Everyone else was so excited about the move to shiny new premises. Some of the staff even lived out that way, and were calculating how much they'd save on petrol on their commute. They were going to have flexi time too, which apparently meant that everyone could have a long weekend. It seemed he was the only one taking redundancy. So far he'd been asked five times to put in a good word for someone who wanted his foreman's job. So far he'd smiled and nodded five times and done nothing.

******

Margaret was so despondent by bedtime that, for a brief moment, she considered chucking her wig into the wardrobe and getting straight into bed. But the habit of years took over and she wearily placed the wig on its stand, cleaned off her makeup, dealt with her contacts, moisturised her skin and tightened her chin strap, all the while thinking resentfully about the unfairness of it all. All I want, she said to herself, is to use my talents. I'm a natural born organiser, I could create the best salon in town and make a lot of money, I know I could, if I didn't have Raymond holding me back. Oh it's alright for him, he only wants to laze about, and he's got that all nice and ready for him.

In the next bedroom Ray was having very similar thoughts, except the organiser/best salon/lot of money bit - but he was definitely feeling cheated. All I want, he said to himself, is a quiet life. I'm not greedy like some people. And how am I going to tell Margaret that we've got to sell the bungalow at a loss, I'll never have another peaceful moment after that.

How am I going to tell Dilys, Margaret was thinking, I promised her a home and a job and she'll get neither. Well she'll just have to make the best of it with Steve I suppose. I'll sleep in the car if I have to but I can't ask her to do that.

******

Across town, alone in bed, Dilys wasn't fed up at all. She'd spent a happy few hours surrounded by clothes and shoes and bags, remembering why she'd bought them or where she'd worn them. There was even the blouse that baby Cheyenne had been sick on at her christening. She had packed everything that had some wear left in it, including the blouse, which might fit one day when the food diary had worked its magic. It wasn't as if Cheyenne had left a stain on it.

FRIDAY APRIL 26th

Margaret didn't often suffer from feelings of guilt, but she knew she should have phoned Dilys straight away yesterday and told her about the loss of the house. She felt even worse when she glanced up from the computer and saw Steve unloading cases and bags from the car. He helped Dilys carry them in and stood awkwardly while she threw herself into Margaret's arms, sobbing.

'It's over,' she wailed, 'he loves his shed more than he loves I!'

Margaret glared at him over Dilys's shoulder. She wasn't speaking to Raymond and it occurred to her now that he and Steve were two of a kind.

'You!' she said, and he froze. 'She's not going to stand for this,' Margaret continued, 'and that's the last time you make her cry. And don't think you can get round her with toffees neither.' It seemed Margaret had remembered their school days after all.

'I were upset,' he said awkwardly, 'that's all. I dunno why she has to carry on so.'

'Is that young Steven?' came Ray's voice from the kitchen. He was used to feelings of guilt, although he mostly ignored them, but he still wasn't quite ready to tell Margaret about the bungalow. He appeared, wiping his hands on a tea towel.

'I thought I heard your dulcet tones. Oh.'

Yes, he'd spotted the women, one sobbing, one furious.

'Give us a lift mate,' he said hastily, 'got a bit of business to see to and Margaret needs the car.'

They left ASAP while Margaret was still wondering whether to tell Ray she didn't, in fact, need the car because she wasn't going in to Kingsford to sign the house agreement. It wasn't guilt so much as denial.

Guilt though had to be dealt with. She had carefully rearranged her Friday morning appointments so that she was free to go to the solicitor's early on, so there was plenty of time to break the news to Dilys before the first client was due mid-morning.

******

'Drop me anywhere, mate,' Ray said, 'I know you need to get to work.'

'Not going,' muttered Steve, 'not going to work, can't face it, finishing at the end of the month anyway. I tell you, Ray, I'm right fed up.

Fed up to me back teeth and out the other side.' He sighed deeply while Ray stared out of the window, embarrassed.

'Tell you what,' Steve said, 'let's go up Minehead.'

'I dunno,' Ray said, 'I'm not in the mood for ice cream with sand in it. You ain't the only one with problems.'

'Nah, I'm thinking of the steam train not the beach. Can't be miserable when you're riding on a steam train.' And he turned the car towards the motorway.

******

Margaret and Dilys were sitting glumly over a coffee when the phone rang. Dilys, when she finally understood about the house and the gold taps and the jacuzzi bath and the dining room and the possible chandelier, had not taken it well. She'd been crying and wailing until Margaret gave her a jam doughnut. She was in no fit state to answer the phone so Margaret grabbed it and before she could speak an excited voice gabbled

'Could I speak to Mrs Richards please? It's, well, it's a personal matter, in a way, yes, personal.'

'How did you get this number?' Margaret asked, feeling she had begun to turn into Dilys's message service.

'Sorry, sorry, I should have said,' the voice said, ' what am I like, I know who you are but you don't know me from Adam, or should I say Eve, anyway, Mrs Richards, this is Tillie from *Happy Ever After* magazine. It's about your story.'

Now Margaret remembered putting the salon number on the covering letter on the basis that Dilys was there more than she was home most of the time. She looked across at Dilys, who was wiping her reddened eyes with a tissue with one hand while holding the doughnut with the other so she could suck the jam out of it between sobs. She decided to hang on to the phone for the moment.

'What about it?' she said.

'We love it. It's wonderful. Food! Love! Happy ending! But the real question is, have you got any more stories like that?'

Margaret looked at Dilys again. Now she was doodling hearts in her notebook while licking the sugar off the doughnut.

'Bottomless pit' she said.

'Wonderful, wonderful. Now Is it possible you could pop up to London on Monday for a little chat? Sign a little agreement maybe? We'd want exclusive access to your material of course. I think you'll find our rates are very fair.'

Margaret could hardly believe what she was hearing. Dilys's silly little story in a magazine, a proper one, not some local newsletter, and paid for to boot. I can't believe it, she thought, here's me, lost everything, and suddenly Dilys gets this. Talk about Not Fair. But she said

'Is eleven o clock suitable to yourselves?'

******

It turned out to be quite true that you can't be miserable on a steam train, specially when the stoker is a friend of one of you and happy to show you how everything works. Sitting back in their carriage later, Ray had recovered from his embarrassment and felt it was time to show his friend some support.

'Tell us about the job then,' he said, 'you ain't been sacked have you?'

'Redundant,' Steve said, 'same thing really.'

'No it's not,' Ray said, 'I been made redundant, you get a lovely little payout and no blot on your copybook, so when you go for another job you got nothing to hide. Coo I wish I had that money now. I wouldn't spend it on a hair salon that's for sure.'

'I was gonna get a new shed with mine,' Steve said, 'bigger, insulated maybe. No point now, council is rehousing us, won't have no garden on the fourth floor. Plus we'll need something to live on pro tem.'

'I wouldn't like a flat,' Ray said, 'poky. On top of each other all the time. That's why I wanted the bungalow, it ain't a palace, but it's big enough for the two of us. Two bedrooms, right, and a room in the roof with…'

'…sea glimpses. You said, the other day. Very nice, you'll like it there.'

'I would have liked it there,' Ray corrected him, 'but now Margaret's ducked out I can't afford it. Even the council tax is beyond belief. I did think of getting a mortgage…'

'You don't want one of they,' Steve said, shocked, 'ball and chain like.'

'Doesn't matter,' Ray said, 'I'm too old anyway, plus how would I afford the repayments? Gonna have to sell it, and on top of that I'll lose a big chunk of money, basically it ain't worth what I paid for it. Tell you what though, why don't you get an allotment? Put the shed on that, bonus is, free veg!'

'Two year wait,' Steve said, 'what you gonna do then? Where you gonna live?'

'Have to rent somewhere I guess. Bedsit maybe.'

'Rarer than hen's teeth round here mate,' Steve said, 'tourist town innum? The grockles gets 'em all.'

Having thoroughly depressed themselves again they fell silent for the rest of the short trip.

******

Dilys struggled to understand what Margaret was saying. She was still preoccupied with the state of her marriage and the loss of the jacuzzi bath.

'London?' she said, 'I can't go can I? Not gonna ask Steve to take me that's for sure. He'd have to leave his shed behind for a whole day. We can't have that can we?' Margaret had no idea that Dilys could do sarcasm. It didn't suit her.

'Never mind about Steve, you don't need him,' she said, 'catch the eight thirty. Let him run you to the station, it's the least he can do.'

'I s'pose' Dilys said, 'big place though, London, scary like.'

'You'll be fine,' Margaret said. She made regular trips to London for visits to a discreet wig maker, which funnily enough always seemed to happen during the Sales. Dilys hadn't been for years.

******

Ray and Steve didn't speak again till they were in the car on their way home.

'You know it's a great shame,' Ray said, 'lovely little garden behind the bungalow. Just right for your shed.'

'If you wasn't selling,' said Steve, 'I could be your lodger. Got a spare room ain't yer?'

******

Margaret was wallowing in despondency. So Raymond gets his bungalow, she thought, without lifting a finger to deserve it, and Dilys gets a little London treat, what do I get? Well at least it can't get any worse.

The phone started ringing. She was reaching for it when Dilys came careering out of the kitchen and picked it up.

'H'Aphrodite's 'Air and Beauty' she said, a tad breathlessly, 'how may I help?' Fair enough, Margaret thought, I did say it had to be answered by the third ring, and she did just about do that. We're getting there.

'H'it's for you, Mrs. Boyles,' Dilys said, in her newly acquired receptionist voice, 'Mr Johnson is h'enquiring if you is available.'

'Oh what now,' Margaret muttered, 'phoning to gloat is he?' She took the phone from Dilys.

'Ah, Mr. Johnson,' she said icily, 'how lovely to hear from you, and so soon after your visit. Were you requiring an appointment after all perhaps? A good cut can do so much for thinning hair.'

Johnson, who was rather proud of his blonde quiff, was rather taken aback. Rich stuff, he thought, coming from a women who I'm almost certain wears a wig (he had been puzzling about Margaret's hair ever since he saw her from the back as she left the restaurant. Something about the hairline made him think it wasn't quite right).

'Very kind of you,' he said drily, 'but of course my ówn salons are always available to me. Whereas you, well, you'll be closing soon won't you.'

There was a silence while they both regrouped.

Johnson had phoned for a reason: he wanted to offer Margaret a job. She was a dreadful woman and therefore exactly what he needed to whip his staff into shape. And Margaret had been wondering how to contact him and persuade him to let her run a small salon somewhere in the area, without actually grovelling. She recovered first and took a deep breath.

'Of course,' she said, 'silly of me. And you have so many salons. Spoilt for choice'

'Indeed indeed,' he said, 'almost too many. Very hard for one man to keep an eye on so many.' The truth was that his second-in-command had unexpectedly resigned, which is a polite way of describing the events of the morning, where she had read his latest memo, called him a cheeseparing skinflint and stormed out, throwing her bunch of keys onto his desk as she left. He had deduced that she wasn't going to implement his latest round of cost cutting measures and he needed a replacement soon, preferably yesterday.

They proceeded to talk over each other.

'So,' Margaret was saying, 'as you know my husband is planning to retire…'

'…He did mention it but you…'

'…Whereas I…'

'…Clearly still so much to offer…'

'…Just a small salon..'

'…I'm in a position to offer you…'

'…Competition is healthy…'

'…a very rare opportunity…'

'...keeps your salons on their toes...'

'...keep my staff on their toes...'

Johnson realised he had no idea what they were talking about. Margaret was quicker on the uptake.

'Are you offering me a job?' she said.

'Of course,' he said, laughing, 'what else would it be? I'd hardly want you to set up in competition would I? But I haven't got room for your trainee, I have a rigorous selection process for staff and she's, well, frankly, and since we're going to work together I will be frank, she's too old and too dumpy.'

Margaret was shocked into silence. She didn't really see Dilys in the moment any more, she saw a mixture of the young pretty Dilys that she used to know, and the slimmer more groomed Dilys that she was currently creating.

'I'm thinking payment by results' he went on, 'we agree a target turnover for a salon and you are rewarded according to your success or otherwise.'

Margaret was imagining herself working for Johnson as his hired trouble shooter and thug. Until the clause expired. Five years. Talk about making a pact with the devil. Maybe there was something worse than a living in a bungalow with Raymond.

Maybe.

'I'll let you know,' she said, and put the phone down, just as the first customer arrived and the afternoon rush started.

******

Margaret and Dilys were wearily clearing up at the end of the day, when Steve and Ray burst in.

'Had a brilliant ideal,' Steve said.

'Your old man's a genius,' Ray said to Dilys, 'well we both are.'

'Gonna rent their spare room,' Steve said.

'Then we won't have to sell the bungalow at a loss.' Ray added.

'You won't have to WHAT?' Margaret said.

SATURDAY APRIL 27th

Ray and Steve spent Saturday at the bungalow. Completion of the purchase was still two days away but Ray wanted to show Steve where he'd be living, the outside anyway. There was nothing to stop them going through the side gate into the back garden to view possible sites for the shed. As they walked up the front path though a woman appeared in the next door garden.

'It's sold,' she said, nodding towards the sign.

'I know,' Ray said, holding out his hand, 'I bought it. I'm your new neighbour, Raymond Boyles, and this…

'Another Brummie retiring down here I suppose,' she said sourly, 'buying up all our houses at ridiculous prices'.

'He's been down here since before you were born,' Steve said hastily, 'practically a native.'

'That's right,' Ray said, withdrawing the hand and rolling out his most charming smile, 'it's so nice to meet you, Mrs?'

'Hang on a mo,' she said, and ducked back inside, emerging almost at once with a biscuit tin.

'You might as well have this now,' she said, passing it across the fence, 'I used to keep an eye out for old Mrs. Williams, feed the cat when she was away with her son, check the mail and so on. It's all yours now. I'm hoping you do something about the state of the back fence, that son of hers was a lazy beggar.'

'I'll see to that,' Steve said, 'right up my street that is.'

The woman was gone, without revealing her name. Inside the tin were keys, some notes about cat feeding, a broken cat collar and a postcard from Sidmouth ('Dear Angela, the weather is dreadful and Godfrey expects me to walk miles and me with my knees. Love to Smudge. Doris.')

They let themselves in, both feeling oddly guilty, like they were scrumping or something. It was some weeks since Ray had viewed the bungalow when it was full of old furniture and knickknacks, and now it was empty he was disoriented. He opened a door, hoping for a bedroom.

'Cupboard,' he said.

'Useful, having a cupboard in the hall,' Steve said, 'why are we whispering?' Ray opened more doors and found the two small bedrooms, the larger living room, the small bathroom and tiny kitchen.

'I like that hatch,' Steve said, 'saves you walking round with stuff.'

'Yup, and you can keep an eye on the TV while you're cooking.'

'Hang on,' Steve said. He pulled out his penknife and opened an attachment, 'hang on a mo, I'm gonna tighten the screw on this here door handle.'

'Margaret says the hatch makes the room look like a cafe,' Ray said, 'she wants it filled in.'

'Wanted,' Steve said, 'do what you like now, mate.' He headed for the stairs.

'Watch yourself,' Ray said, 'it ain't a proper staircase. Not to building regs or some such. Another reason we got it cheap. The upstairs room don't count see? Not without a proper staircase.'

'Seems sturdy enough,' Steve said, 'and we could soon rig up a better handrail.'

The upstairs room, which covered the entire footprint of the building, seemed enormous but not in a good way. The sloping walls made it hard to stand up round the edges, and the single dormer window, the source of the sea glimpses, didn't let in much light. There was ancient lino on the floor that was full of holes and a lingering smell that suggested mice or worse.

'I was wondering,' Ray said, 'if you'd like this room. Fix it up like a sort of bedsit, with your own telly and so on. Bit of privacy up here.' Steve turned to him with shining eyes.

'Really?' he said, 'you'd really give I the best room in the house? Oh, Ray, I could put me layout up here, build a bench all round right, raise it up to a convenient height, stations, sidings, tunnel maybe. Or a viaduct, always wanted a viaduct. No more putting it away and getting it out, everything set up permanent like.'

'I suppose you could, but won't you want furniture? Wardrobe, chest of drawers, that sort of thing?'

'Nah, keep it all in carrier bags under the bench. Only got the one suit, it can have a hook on the door. Bed in the middle right? Hinged flap across the doorway for the track, have to rehang the door to open out of course, not a problem. Perfect in fact. Oh, Ray I could hug yer.'

'Alright alright, don't get carried away.'

******

Dilys was so miserable her empowerment seemed to have melted away like snow in summer. She forgot to turn the kettle on and served several customers with stone cold coffee. She washed a customer's hair in conditioner instead of shampoo - Margaret noticed in time and passed it off as 'one of our new treatments'. Dilys was about to rinse it off with the hydrogen peroxide they used for bleaching hair when Margaret called a halt before any serious harm came to a customer. She sent Dilys to the kitchen to calm down and twenty minutes later found her sitting at the table staring into space, a half-eaten doughnut in front of her. This was clearly serious. She vaguely remembered one of the talks at the women's weekend, something to do with being kinder to staff. 'An ounce of empathy is worth more than a ton of anger'. Or something. Her instinct was more of the pull yourself together type of thing but she decided to give it a go.

'What's up?' she said as kindly as she could (she was very out of practice), 'don't worry about the conditioner thing, the bottles are really quite similar. Apart from the colour. And the size.' Dilys shook her head.

'Yeah,' she said, 'sorry.' And she fell silent again. I'll give this one more go, Margaret thought, and then I'll have to get back into the salon whether she likes it or not. They'll be growing restless out there.

'I can't go up London,' Dilys said sadly, 'it's too big and it's too noisy and what am I gonna wear? They'll laugh at I in this old dress. I ain't doing it, Margie, I just ain't.'

'Oh yes you are,' said Margaret, relieved to have something practical to get her teeth into, 'you wrote that story and you deserve to see it in the magazine. All of London is big, yes, but you aren't going to all of it, just one little bit. Try to think of it as a load of villages joined together, that's what I always do. I'll lend you my *A to Z* so you don't get lost and tomorrow we'll work out the best clothes for you so that you're simultaneously comfortable and smart. But right now, Dilys we have clients waiting. Come along, we've got a job to do. Chin up, and don't forget to smile.'

To Margaret's surprise this worked. Dilys stood up, squared her shoulders, picked up her doughnut and took a large bite, and marched out to the salon.

******

Ray's back was giving him gyp. He had wondered why Steve had a ladder tied to the roof of his car and now he knew. It was so you could check the gutters. He was beginning to feel rebellious. I never checked the gutters on the salon he thought, and I don't see why I should start now. But there was Steve up the ladder, while Ray at the bottom was footing it in a most awkward position that his poor back didn't like one little bit.

'Coming down,' Steve called out. 'Roof looks sound enough,' he said when he was safely back in the ground, 'but them gutters is chock-a-block. Have to do something about that won't we.'

'They'll be fine,' Ray muttered. He didn't notice Steve's shocked expression. Steve was beginning to suspect that his old friend was a tad lazy. Just a tad.

******

There was a lull in the early afternoon and Margaret sent Dilys off to the kitchen to make herself a sandwich. Then she phoned Barbara.

'Listen,' she said, 'I need your help. Dilys needs a makeover toot sweet, so I was wondering if we could come round to your flat on Sunday and go through her clothes. I haven't got room here to spread them out but we could do it in your dining room.'

'Why,' said Barbara sourly, 'is she up in court?'

'Oh don't be like that,' Margaret said, 'come on be a pal.' There was a silence at the other end so she pressed on. 'Did I tell you about my new treatment idea?'

'No.'

'Well, it's a little sideline I'm starting up and Dilys is testing it for me.'

'Oh,' Barbara said, 'I could have done that.' Margaret laughed.

'It's for women with grooming and weight issues,' she said, 'I couldn't test it on someone with no issues now could I?' This was an unintentional stroke of genius because Barbara was immediately mollified and intrigued, and she did love playing around with clothes.

'Well there's nothing happening on Sunday, it's a golf day so I'll be home alone. But why the big rush?'

'You won't believe this,' Margaret said, 'in fact I hardly believe it myself, but on Monday morning she has to go to London to see about selling a story to *Happy Ever After* magazine. She's been wearing her funeral dress for work and…' Now Barbara was laughing.

'You mean the one she'll be buried in?'

'Very funny. Could you pick us up about ten? Ray keeps helping himself to the car and we'll have all her suitcases.'

SUNDAY APRIL 28th

Sunday morning Ray left early to carry on planning his new life with Steve. He had intended a quiet Sunday morning with the sports pages and a can of beer, instead of the usual salon cleaning ritual, but Steve wanted to measure up for the new shed he was planning. The idea now was that he would do all the maintenance work on the trains in the shed keeping his room for the permanent layout, and perhaps even start his own little repair business. Plenty of model railway enthusiasts didn't have the first idea how to repair and rebuild a locomotive, something which always astonished him. He was full of ideas and kept distracting Ray with them - there was the question of running power out to the shed ('do it properly this time, so's I can have a decent heater'), insulating it maybe, and finding an old rug for the floor ('sick and tired of cold feet all winter').

'Tell you what,' he said, as he paced out the back garden, 'reckon there's room here for a proper garage. Look, it's wide enough for a driveway down the side 'ere, right, then once you get past the house and it's a bit wider you can put a nice little garage right here, near the kitchen door and...' Ray looked up from his paper.

'I ain't planning any home improvements,' he said, 'this is retirement not work.'

'Oh it wouldn't be much, you can even buy 'em ready to go, prefab like,' Steve said, 'concrete slab, crane it in, Bob's your uncle, sorted. Anyway you can't do nothing, it ain't natural.'

'Oh yeah?' said Ray, 'just you watch me.' Shaking his head, Steve gave Ray the end of the tape measure to hold. Ray put the loop at the end over his finger so he could still hold the paper with two hands, but when he turned the page Steve yelled out 'keep still can't you, I'm measuring here.' It seemed an endless business, with many notes on a scrap of paper, so Ray gave up on the newspaper and settled for a little snooze instead.

******

Margaret hardly noticed Ray leaving, she was so engrossed in remodelling Dilys's hair into something sleeker and altogether more controlled. Dilys didn't object, she was still stunned by the twin ideas of selling her story, for real money, to a real magazine and not being with Steve any more. She allowed Margaret to pull her curls into a sort of helmet shape, held in place with extra strong hairspray. She didn't even object to the idea of spending the day with that spiky Barbara sort, and she climbed into the back seat of the car without a murmur. And then Barbara announced her surprise.

'Don't bother with all those suitcases, ' she said, 'we're meeting Clover at the Little Dress Shop, she's going to let us in and leave us till lunchtime. She does that occasionally for a trusted customer.'

'She's never let me do that!' Margaret said enviously, 'still it's an excellent idea. We could find Dilys a smart little suit, so that she looks businesslike. We want them to take her seriously.'

After an hour or so they realised there wasn't much in Dilys's size, apart from a grey suit with a pencil skirt that luckily looked as if it might do. Margaret had brought with her a pair of her own smart heels, because despite the weight difference they did take the same size in shoes.

It took a while but eventually they wedged/dressed Dilys in the suit, complete with a pale blue blouse with pussy cat bow. Barbara was in her element, tweaking and fiddling until everything was just right. She forgot all about being jealous of Dilys. She'd always loved playing dress up with her dolls.

With her flattened hair, and false eyelashes, and balanced on Margaret's three inch heels Dilys looked quite the thing Margaret thought, pleased with all their hard work.

'I feels like a right numpty,' Dilys said glumly, looking in the mirror.

'Yes,' said Barbara thoughtfully, 'we're not there yet. The thing is, Margaret, she's a little bit..'

'Plump? I know,' said Margaret, 'but we're working on that, aren't we, Dilly?'

'No,' said Barbara, 'plump is neither here nor there, we work with what we've got, right? No, what I'm saying is, she's not really the grey suit type, she's more... boho. That's it, boho, like she time travelled from the Summer of Love. I'm thinking flowery. I'm thinking shawls. I'm thinking bangles up the arm. I'm thinking...' she leaned forward and seized Dilys on either side of her head, ruffling her hair back into its natural crazy curls, then she wrapped a large fringed embroidered shawl around her. Inspired, Dilys kicked off the shoes and put her trainers back on.

'Doc Martens,' said Barbara, 'that place in the covered market is open Sundays. And some wooden beads? Or big earrings maybe? Anyway, ditch the two piece, we want a long colourful skirt, elastic waist of course, plain top, shawl, jewellery.'

She ran into the back of the shop and quickly returned with a flowery skirt from the unsellables rack.

'Oh,' said Margaret once Dilys was re-dressed, 'I see what you mean, that look does suit her, but is that right for a business meeting? She needs to impress them, they need to know she can deliver the goods. She needs to look the part so they don't patronise her, you know what they're like up there.'

'That's your job ' said Barbara, 'you are going with her aren't you?' In the course of the morning she had warmed to Dilys, and she also felt a creator's pride in the finished product and she didn't want London to ruin it.

'Oh yes, please come with us, Marge,' Dilys said, 'I hates the thought of going up London on my own.'

'Well,' said Margaret weakly, for she did love a trip to London, 'the thing is, I've got my pensioners…'

'Phone them,' Barbara said crisply, 'tell them something unavoidable came up. Good grief, Margaret, you can't throw Dilys to the wolves. They'll eat her alive. You'll dress smart, of course, but Dilys should be colourful. And don't let her sign anything. Oh, and you can borrow John's attaché case, Mother gave it to him at Christmas but he refuses to use it. Prefers his old leather thing. Men eh?'

MONDAY APRIL 29th

They caught the early train to London, Margaret in her smartest suit and Dilys togged out in the shawl and flowery skirt combo with her curls flying madly round her head. She loved the new clothes but they hadn't done anything at all for her self-confidence. In fact she was so anxious she hadn't been able to eat any breakfast, only the second time that had ever happened, the first being when she was in labour with Cheyenne. She sat staring out of the window as the countryside rushed by, chewing the side of her lip. Margaret was busy with the tube map in her AtoZ. Her knowledge of London was confined to certain shopping streets and her wig makers, and the *Happy Ever After* office was in an area she had never even heard of, so in the end they took a taxi. Margaret made a note of the cost of it. She had a vague idea of docking Dilys's future wages to cover their expenses, although even she could see that wasn't quite the right thing to do.

******

Steve and Ray were sitting in the Reception area of Furkins Furkins and Furkins looking sheepish. They'd been sheepish since first thing, when Ray dropped Margaret off at the station at the same time as Steve arrived with Dilys. Margaret had buttonholed them both simultaneously, and made it quite clear that

a) they were not to trespass on the bungalow any more until after the completion at midday ('can't trespass on your own property' Ray had muttered rebelliously, but also very, very, quietly.)

b) Ray was not to take a tenant into her half of the bungalow without her permission and

c) they were to get themselves off to the solicitor and put the whole thing on a proper footing.

Steve objected that he had to get to work, and then remembered that he didn't care about that any more. Even so, he felt very strange being out and about on a Monday. Like the kind of dream where you've forgotten your pants and you're walking down the street naked.

Miss Dollymore, who was finding it harder and harder to say 'Mr Simpkins' when she was now used to calling him Perry, had said 'I'll see if he's free' and had disappeared into the office for a good twenty minutes, coming out at last with her hair somewhat tousled and the information that 'he'll be with you shortly.'

Perry, sorry, Mr. Simpkins, didn't think much of the bungalow sharing idea, but suggested if they must do it there should be a six month trial period, laid out by himself in a simple but legal format.

'And hang on to that offer from the council for now,' he said to Steve, 'you don't want to end up homeless if things don't work out.'

******

By soon after eleven Margaret and Dilys were seated in Tillie's office with a coffee. Margaret was surprised to find that a London magazine editor was even more boho than Dilys. She even had tattoos - she'll regret that in a few years, when everything goes all wrinkly and saggy, Margaret thought, but she didn't say anything. She also didn't mention that she'd impersonated Dilys on the phone, and Tillie didn't seem to notice the difference.

'So, Mrs. Richards,' said Tillie, once the introductions were done 'or may I call you Dilys? I always think it's nicer to be on first name terms, you must call me Tillie of course.'

Dilys turned and looked imploringly at Margaret, who nodded.

'Yes please,' said Dilys.

'Well as I said on the phone, we did rather like your little story. You have a very unusual and rather refreshing approach. Rather fun, I ran it past the girls in the office and they all liked it. But you are a new author, and we can only really commit to you if you can continue to supply stories on a regular basis. Do you think you can do that? One a month say? And you think you can maintain the quality? That's very important, our readers soon complain if there's any dropping off.'

Dilys looked at Margaret.

'We wouldn't want to flood the market,' Margaret said, 'Mrs Richards is looking to establish a career. She has plenty of material of course, and she is fully computerised.'

Dilys choked on her coffee.

'Wonderful,' beamed Tillie, 'in that case, Dilys, I would suggest two pen names. Many of our authors have two names. Of course then you would need two distinct story styles. You could keep one name for the food and love stories but what would you do for the other name?'

She looked at Dilys.

Dilys looked at Margaret.

'Mrs Richards has already established her food and love approach,' Margaret said grandly, steadfastly ignoring the first name nonsense, 'so I suggest we start with that. We have one or two other ideas in development but they're still at an early stage.'

'Fine, fine,' said Tillie, 'I'll leave that one with you, as long as you keep 'em coming. Now here is our style sheet, as you can see the story you sent us was only just long enough. Word count is extremely important, so I suggest you aim for the upper end, that way if we need to prune anything we can. We do have to be mindful of our readers' sensitivities and our writers can't be expected to understand the detail of all that.'

She offered the paper to Dilys.

Margaret took it.

'Finally,' Tillie said, 'the small matter of our contract. I expect you'd like your business manager to have a quick read through?' Dilys looked all round the room as if expecting a business manager to pop out from behind a filing cabinet.

'She means me,' Margaret hissed. She took the contract and put it in the attaché case along with the style sheet.

'We'll have our legal advisor check it out,' she said, closing the case firmly, 'and let you know in due course. Come, Dilys, we have things to do.'

She stood to leave, shook hands with a slightly stunned Tillie and strode out, with Dilys trotting after her.

******

Steve and Ray were walking round Kingsford killing time before they, or at least Ray, was due back at Furkins, Furkins and Furkins for the formal completion of the purchase plus collection of the keys at midday. Steve was examining the houses, with particular reference to the garages. He'd never been to Kingsford before and he wasn't a big fan of quaint country villages.

'Too small,' he said, 'everyone knows your business like, nothing private, ooh, what about that!'

That was a new house squeezed onto a tiny plot between two older houses with a garage sideways on in the front garden.

'Perfect,' Steve said, 'just what the doctor ordered. We can put a nice little garage in the front and leave the back free.'

'For your shed I suppose,' Ray said.

'And your deckchair,' Steve said.

******

Margaret had daydreamed about a London shopping spree after lunch, but she knew she didn't have any money to spare, so she hustled them back to Paddington and the next train home.

Relief set Dilys chattering. Margaret was trying to think through what had happened. Was it really possible that Dilys was going to be a writer and Margaret was going to be her business manager? It looked easy enough but... no. No. She was a hairdresser and beautician. She would find a way to get a new salon, if she had to move to Timbuctoo to do it. (She had decided that she wouldn't work for Johnson, and was planning to phone him when she got home). Writing stories could be a nice little hobby for Dilys, that's all.

'She were a funny one, that Tillie,' Dilys was saying, 'did you see her tattoos? One them was a heart with an arrow through, I could get one of they couldn't I? 'Course, my heart is broken, I reckons I could get a broken heart one, big crack right down the middle with tears coming out. They never give us a biscuit with that coffee, has you got any bikkies in that case thing, Marge? Or a choccie bar?'

'They'll be round with the snacks and sandwiches in a minute,' Margaret said, 'then you can have some lunch. In the meantime why don't you start your next story?' She needed peace and quiet to work out what she could say to Johnson that might persuade him to drop the five year clause. She pulled a new notebook and a pen out of her case and pushed them across to Dilys, who was suddenly looking stricken.

'How can I do a new story?' she said, 'you know it weren't a proper story, just my food diary gone mad. And now me and Steve... me and Steve...' The tears were coming. Margaret quickly gave her a tissue.

'I'm sure you can think of something,' she said, 'do one about, oh I don't know, what about when you were young? When you were courting?'

'Ooh I know,' Dilys said, 'how about when we was in Majorca, lovely that was, I remember watching my Steve eating his chips on the beach...'

'No!' said Margaret, her hand involuntarily going up to check her wig, 'not Majorca for goodness sake.' But it was too late, Dilys had seized the pen and was scribbling away, leaving Margaret to wonder gloomily if her terrible experience was going to feature in Dilys's new story. So much for not getting involved.

'When we get home I'll type it up for you,' she said kindly, but she was thinking 'if there's any mention of candles or fire extinguishers it's going straight in the bin.'

******

It was done. Properly done at last. Ray had the keys safe in his pocket. The bungalow was his. With Steve on board the expenses were near enough covered. It was time to celebrate.

******

By the time they got off the train Margaret had decided her best policy was to let the whole story thing die a quiet death. It wasn't as if Dilys cared one way or the other about it, unlike Margaret herself with her salon. She was definitely going to try and charm Johnson into letting her have her salon, although the details were still a little vague. However she had reckoned without the restorative power of two limp cheese sandwiches, stale salt and vinegar crisps and a small packet of custard creams.

'Let's go straight up that solicitors,' Dilys said eagerly, 'we ain't got no old ladies s'afternoon and I ain't seen young Dolly in an age. I wonder if her's courting yet.'

'Oh no rush,' said Margaret, who would prefer it if the contract wasn't signed at all, 'they'll be closing soon I expect.'

'S'only three o' clock' said Dilys, 'and there's a bus at ten past. Oooh, tell you what, let's get another taxi, that were right fun, all them stories he told us about famous people.'

'That is not going to happen in Weston-super-Mare,' said Margaret, 'and don't start spending the money before you've earned it. We'll go on the bus.' (She had every intention of missing the bus).

They were walking across the station forecourt when Ray pulled up.

'Margaret,' he yelled, 'jump in quick, we've got to…'

'I'm busy,' Margaret said.

'Never mind,' Dilys said, 'you go with Ray, I'll get the bus on me own.'

Margaret hesitated, wondering how she could stop Dilys. The Dilys who was standing right in front of her full of excitement, holding her hand out for the case. And just like that she gave in. To hell with it she thought, why shouldn't Dilys have something for herself. Let her publish her little story, I probably won't even be a hairdresser this time next year so why should I care. She proffered the attaché case.

'Make sure he checks every word,' she said, 'I'm not having you ripped off, right?'

******

'This had better be good, Raymond,' Margaret said as they drove through the town at breakneck speed.

'You forgot your pensioners!' Ray gabbled, 'luckily me and Steve were just back from the pub and...'

'I most certainly did not forget them. I cancelled them.'

'We found them on the doorstep, trying to get into the salon...'

'I simply phoned Miss Stibb and asked her to be kind enough to notify the others.'

'I had to let them in, and make some excuse, then I took a chance on you being on the three o' clock train, luckily I'd only had a half, new policy, money's tight, I couldn't let Steve drive, he's been wetting the baby's head, you know, his new layout, so I told him to keep them amused like Dilys did, then I...'

'RAYMOND!'

'What?'

'Was Miss Stibb there?'

'Um, dunno, which one is she?'

As they pushed open the door of the salon they heard Steve's voice 'Now the 000 gauge you see, is quite a different matter...'

******

As Dilys pushed open the door of Furkins, Furkins and Furkins all she could hear was sobbing. An elderly woman dressed in tweeds was sitting on a chair crying and clutching a large cat basket. The cat inside appeared to be asleep, or dead. The woman was vaguely familiar but Dilys was too preoccupied to look closely.

'Oh,' she said, 'is there a queue?'

Miss Dollymore looked up from her screen.

'Oh hello, Mrs Richards,' she said, 'I ain't seen you in an age. Was you wanting to see Per... Mr. Simpkins? It's alright, Mrs. Hetherington is taking a moment to compose herself. You can go right in.'

Dilys went right in. On the bus, bracing herself for the meeting, she'd remembered the visit Simpkins had paid to the salon. She'd always thought a solicitor was a scary old man with half-moon glasses but this one was young, in fact he looked about twelve. It was easy for the new Dilys, empowerment restored by the triumphant trip to London, to ask him 'is this 'ere OK?' and hand over the papers.

Rather absently he started to read the Style Sheet. He was still recovering from a bruising call with his mother at lunchtime. Dolly had urged him to 'get it over and done with', so he did. It appeared that his mother didn't approve of chickens. She wasn't quite sure what a bantam was, some sort of pugilist perhaps, but she was sure she didn't approve of them either. Luckily his legal training came to his aid, and he reminded her in tremulous tones that he was an adult and her approval was not required. There was a silence, then his father came on the line and told him that Mummy had fainted.

Then Mrs. Hetherington and Pooky had appeared, full of outrage (her) and sedatives (him). After a difficult hour he reminded her that his time had to be paid for and she finally gave up.

'Well,' he said to Dilys wearily, 'I suppose it's OK but I'm never entirely sure about apostrophes myself. Would you like me to look into it for you?' She blushed, retrieved the style sheet and gave him the contract.

He said he'd look it over and be in touch shortly. What he really meant was he'd check with Furkins, who had specialised in copyright law when his wife decided to write a book about beekeeping.

Once that was all over Dilys really fancied a bit of a catchup with Dolly but Mrs. Hetherington was still there. She seemed to have recovered the power of speech.

'It hardly seems possible,' she said with a sigh, 'that in this day and age an insurance company would be so hard hearted as to expect me to go on a world cruise when poor dear Pooky is convalescing. I suppose that young man *is* fully qualified?'

'Of course he is,' said Miss Dollymore fiercely 'he's the best there is.'

Hello, thought Dilys, summat going on there I reckon.

'Well it simply does not make any sense to me,' said Mrs Hetherington, 'I am covered for the illness or death of a close family member, well what is Pooky if not that? Oh just an animal apparently. Just an animal! And now it seems I shall not have my World Cruise, with balcony and platinum drinks and dining, and I shall also lose all the money I paid for it. How can that be right? It doesn't make any sense. No sense at all.'

******

Margaret was cashing up, a simple process when all you'd done was soothe five old ladies by giving them a free shampoo and set, and fielding their constant demands for a story. It turned out that Miss Stibb was growing rather forgetful, and had simply forgotten to tell the others it was cancelled, and then forgotten all about it and turned up herself anyway.

Margaret had sent Ray to drive Steve home and was enjoying the peace and quiet of an empty salon when Dilys arrived, wreathed in smiles and excitement.

'Marge, Marge,' she squealed, 'oh Marge, you'll never believe it, I seen that Mrs. 'Etherington…'

'I have no desire to discuss that woman,' Margaret said, 'please refrain from mentioning her again.'

'Well her cat…'

'The same applies to that wretched cat.'

Dilys's face softened.

'Ah, poor thing,' she said, 'he's right been in the wars. Look, he scratched I'. She held out her hand, which had an angry looking red line across it.

'You should sue,' Margaret said, 'supposing it turns septic?'

'Oh it's nothing,' said Dilys, 'that's only a little scratch from when I give him his tablet.'

'You what!'

'Give him his tablet. I seen them up the solicitor's, ooh, guess what, I reckon him and Dolly is on the road to love…'

'DILYS!'

'Sorry. So she says he weren't taking his tablets like a good boy, and so I went up her house…'

'You did what!'

'I went up her house and I showed her how to give him his tablet, remember how mum used to do it, you has to know where to press at the side of their little faces, she were always doing the cats in our street, did yours I expect.'

'We never had a cat.'

'You sure? I thought you had that little black one. Or was it a tabby?'

'Dilys, for goodness sake tell me what's going on.'

'Oh OK, sorry. Well. I went up her house and pressed on his little face, after he scratched me and I remembered to wrap him in a towel, and his mouth popped open, and Mrs. 'Etherington put the tablet in and I closed his mouth and I held it shut till he swallowed, then she give me a cupper tea and a cruise.'

'She gave you WHAT!'

'Cupper tea. Oh and a ginger nut. And a cruise. So we're leaving next week.'

For the first time ever Margaret was completely and utterly speechless. She stared at Dilys. She opened her mouth. But no sounds came out of it. Not so much as a croak. In fact she could barely breathe. Dilys began to feel uncomfortable.

'You OK, Marge? You ain't doing shock like that time in Majorca?' Margaret shook her head.

'Good,' said Dilys, 'cos that were a rum do and no mistake. See, she couldn't get her money back on the insurance, so she give it to me as a thank you for me and a sorry about the house for you, we phoned them and everything, instead of a posh suite with two rooms and a balcony for one old lady we got an ordinary cabin for two of us for the same money but no window but we got a shower and a toilet just for us. And oh, Marge, guess what, it stops in Australia, we can see Cheyenne! And palm trees!' Margaret swallowed hard and forced some words out.

'I can't go,' she managed, 'I… I've got to get a new salon. And somewhere to live. And… and…'

'It's only four months,' Dilys said, 'Ray and Steve can have the bungalow, when we gets back we can work out what to do. And oh, think of the stories I can write. I can do a whole load about love on cruises, and I'm gonna call myself Divora O'Hara, like that Scarlet but Divora instead see?'

Margaret had always wanted to go on a cruise. It was her single biggest dream, to go on a luxury cruise and be waited on hand, foot and finger. For years she had buried the dream, but now it surged out of its hiding place and overwhelmed her. It was unbearable. She had to go.

'I don't know, Dilys,' she said slowly, 'it's just that, if we're sharing a cabin… there's something we need to sort out.' She took a deep deep breath and let it out slowly just like the yoga woman on the empowerment weekend taught her. 'It's… about… my… hair…'

'It looks fine,' Dilys said, 'it doesn't need a trim yet,' (Margaret was wearing the middle wig) 'funny though how it grows down so even all over, mine always grows quicker at the sides, and Steve's grows quicker at the front, but yours…'

'Oh, Dilys,' Margaret sighed 'Stop pretending. Just stop. Stop it. You know it's a wig. You know I wear a wig, ever since that time in Majorca.'

'What, with the candle?' Margaret repressed the great sob that was building somewhere in her chest. She breathed again, slowly, slowly.

'Yes, the time with the candle. It never grew back, not properly, and who's going to patronise a hairdresser with hair like bum fluff?'

Dilys threw her arms round her friend.

'Oh, Marge, I'm so sorry. I never knew. But it's only hair, Margie, it's only hair. Tell you what, I'll go and put the kettle on. You got any cake?'

THE END

EPILOGUE

Some of you have kindly pointed out that I appear to have written 'ideal' when I intended 'idea'. It's not a mistake, it's how we say it down here. Lovely job.

Printed in Great Britain
by Amazon